A. J. Mounteney Jephson

Stories Told in an African Forest by Grown-Up Children of Africa

A. J. Mounteney Jephson

Stories Told in an African Forest by Grown-Up Children of Africa

ISBN/EAN: 9783337119867

Printed in Europe, USA, Canada, Australia, Japan

Cover: Foto ©Andreas Hilbeck / pixelio.de

More available books at **www.hansebooks.com**

STORIES TOLD IN AN AFRICAN

FOREST

BY GROWN-UP CHILDREN OF AFRICA.

BY

A. J. MOUNTENEY JEPHSON,

One of Mr. Stanley's officers; and Author of "Emin Pasha and the
Rebellion at the Equator."

With numerous Illustrations from drawings by

WALTER W. BUCKLEY.

LONDON:

SAMPSON LOW, MARSTON & COMPANY,

LIMITED.

St. Dunstan's House.

Fetter Lane, Fleet Street.

1893.

CHISWICK PRESS :—C. WHITTINGHAM AND CO., TOOKS COURT,
CHANCERY LANE.

I DEDICATE

THIS LITTLE BOOK

TO

MY TWENTY-NINE NEPHEWS AND NIECES!

PREFACE.

IN offering this little book to the public I feel that I ought also to offer with it a short explanation and apology.

An explanation of how it came to be written at all, and an apology for calling it a book, when it is scarcely more than a few little sketches strung together.

It was written originally as a series of articles for a children's magazine.

When I was travelling last year in America I was asked by an editor of a magazine to write some short articles on Africa for children. At his rather urgent request I consented, and wrote the following little sketches, most of which are taken from some of the common Zanzibar stories such as are told by the men in almost every African caravan.

For various reasons I withdrew them from publication in the magazine, but at the request of some of my friends who liked them I now publish them in the form of this little book.

11, St. James's Place, London,
         September, 1892.

CONTENTS.

LIST OF FULL-PAGE ILLUSTRATIONS.

STORIES TOLD IN AN AFRICAN FOREST BY GROWN-UP CHILDREN.

CHAPTER I.

INTRODUCTORY.

SOME time ago, when I was in America, I was asked to write some stories for children. I hardly knew what to write about, for American children know so much more than English children, and therefore it is a good deal harder to write for them. I recollect telling some stories to some little American children who constantly wanted to know the reason for everything I told them ; and that was just what I was not always able to do.

My first experience of the precocity of American children

was, I remember, on board ship on my way to the United States. I was watching a sailor drawing water in a bucket from the sea, and asked a bystander what he was doing. A little American boy of eight years old heard my question and answered in a pitying tone, " Oh, don't you know ? We are now in the Gulf Stream, that sailor is drawing water in order to take the temperature and write it down in the Log Book." I immediately "took a back seat," feeling ashamed that my ignorance should have been so apparent to that small boy.

And so I asked myself " What can I write about in order to satisfy American children ? " I cannot tell them stories of "ologies" and "isms," as cousin Cram-child or Professor Huxley would.

But the idea of writing something for children has been put into my head. So I will try if I can to interest English children by telling them about the life of a little band of men who were closed in for many months in a great dark forest in the heart of Africa.

Yes, shut off far away from civilization and home, knowing nothing of what was going on in the outside world, surrounded by hostile tribes of savage cannibals and hordes of vicious, spiteful little dwarfs, who were ever ready to attack, with their poisoned arrows, any one whom they found wandering far from our camp.

I might tell you about our life there, of our work, and how we cleared the land and planted Indian corn and beans; of some of our experiences with these spiteful little pigmies, and of the troops of elephants which used to

"WE MADE AND MENDED OUR CLOTHES AND BOOTS."

come into our fields at night to eat and destroy our crops. I can tell you also of how we built our Fort; how we made and mended our clothes and boots; how we listened to the strange allegorical legends told us by our men (our faithful Negroes), and of all that we hoped and feared and suffered. How would this do?

Well, I will begin from the time when we first came to that part of the country, and I hope before long I shall be able to interest you young people, and give you a glimpse of the hard-working adventurous life we led in that great forest, far away from home.

Our party consisted of Mr. Stanley with his little fox terrier dog Randy, who was the faithful companion of his master. Then there were Captain Stairs, Captain Nelson, Dr. Parke and myself (four young Englishmen who had gone out as officers under Mr. Stanley).

With us were about 200 black men; not like the Negroes in America, who have been spoilt by civilization, and give themselves airs of equality with the white men—I may almost say of superiority. No! our Negroes were not like them, their faces were similar, but their hearts were quite different. Neither did they dress in fine European clothes, as the American Negroes do, but they dressed only in the white or coloured cotton clothes they were accustomed to in their own country—and very nice they looked in them, too, for they were far prettier and more suitable to the hot climate.

Our Negroes were simple-hearted, good-natured, bois-terous people, who looked up to us as their head and loved to work with us, for they knew that we cared for them, and trusted them and treated them kindly. They used to work hard for us and bring us food, and then when work was over and the day was done, they would come and sit round the camp fires with us as we smoked our pipes in the evenings, gossiping and talking and dancing as merrily as if they were children.

They told us stories about the Arab caravans with which they had travelled; about the wonderful countries and people they had seen in their wanderings, or about their wives and homes in the far-off island of Zanzibar.

They were a primitive, kindly, ignorant people, who did not know a word of English and could not read. They were never able even to catch our names, and so they invented nick-names which they thought suited us.

Mr. Stanley they called Bula Matari, or the Rock-breaker, because years before when he was cutting the roads by the river Congo he used to make his men break stones for paving. They called Captain Stairs, who had our big Maxim gun under his charge, Bwana Mazinga, or the Master of the Cannon. Captain Nelson, who was a big, tall fellow, they named Pandalamona, or the Big-Strong man. Doctor Parke received the nick-name of Bwana Doctari, or Mr. Doctor; while I was named Bubarika, or the Chetah, because they said I was so headstrong and

rash. Each European had his nick-name and was always
known to our Negroes by that name. I remember hearing
on the Congo there was a white man who had rather a
bad temper and used to make a tremendous noise when
he blew his nose. Well, the Negroes immediately named
him Barragourm, or the War Horn. Sometimes, early on
a still morning, when he came out of his tent, he could
be heard in the distance, blowing his nose, and the men
would immediately call to each other, " Look out, boys !
Mind what you are about ! Here comes the War Horn ! "
And so, except among ourselves, we never heard our own
names.

But, dear me ! How forgetful I am, I have not told
you yet how it was that we came to be in Africa at
all.

Well, we had gone out there to rescue a brave man
called Emin Pasha, who was surrounded by hostile tribes
in a distant country on the river Nile.

Years before, the Mahdi, who was the False Prophet of
the Soudan, had killed the noble General Gordon and
taken the great town of Khartoum. Emin Pasha was one
of General Gordon's officers, and was Governor of a
country called Hatlastiva. It was in this country that he
was attacked by the Mahdi and found himself unable to
retreat. Nothing had been heard of Emin Pasha for years,

and everyone thought he was dead, when suddenly one day news reached England that he had beaten back the Mahdi and was still alive, but was in great danger.

The English people at once got up an expedition to carry him help, and Mr. Stanley said he would lead it, so we were now on our way to rescue Emin Pasha from the clutches of the Mahdi.

Our path had led through a trackless forest, where we suffered terribly from hunger and sickness ; we had been obliged to eat toad-stools and fungus—blue, green and yellow—which we picked from the rotten stumps of trees. Our men ate dried caterpillars, and slugs, and nasty bitter beans like horse-chestnuts ; and it was a wonder that we were not all poisoned by the things we ate. We had one donkey with us belonging to Mr. Stanley, and at last, when we were almost starving, we killed it. It was very tough, and did not taste at all nice, but we were so hungry we did not care, and ate it all up, from its nose to its tail. And so we struggled on, and at last emerged from the forest, and came upon a huge clearing planted with bananas. In this clearing we found a large village called Ibwiri; it had been deserted by the natives, and here we determined to stay and rest awhile, and recover our strength before moving on. And now I have told you how it was we came to be in Africa and to build our village, which we called Fort Bodo, or the Peaceful Fort, and I will now go on to tell you how we built it.

First of all we measured off a large space shaped like a diamond, and fenced it in with a strong, high palisade of young saplings, to defend ourselves against the attacks of the savages. Round this fence we dug a broad, deep ditch, and put thorns in the bottom of it, so that if the savages tried to get over it they would prick their feet and legs, for they were quite naked and wore no boots. Then we built four high watch towers at each corner of the fort, and put two men in them each day and night so that they could look round and see that no enemy approached ; they had guns, too, to shoot at the savages if they tried to get into the Fort. And when we had done this we made ourselves mud huts and thatched them with leaves, and then we began to feel snug and comfortable, and turned our attention to clearing the forest and making fields in which to plant corn and beans.

One party of men cut down the thick underwood and tangled masses of creepers which covered the ground, while another carried away the rubbish and burned it in large bonfires.

We worked from six in the morning till six at night, and only had an hour's rest at midday. The sun was broiling hot and it was very hard work, but the men were cheery

FORT BOISÉ.

and gay-hearted, and lightened their labour by singing their Zanzibar songs which were exceedingly enlivening and tuneful.

One man would sing a song, the words of which he made up as he went along, while his companions joined in the chorus, keeping time with their axes and hoes.

It is, of course, impossible to translate their songs—which they would keep up for an hour at a time—exactly into English, but the following doggerel verses may give you some idea of the way the songs went. The chorus was "Nainda-Shamba-Kulima," which means "Go to the fields and hoe," and the chorus was sung very short and staccato.

ZANZIBAR FIELD SONG.

We passed through the gloomy forest—
Chorus   Go to the fields and hoe.
Many a comrade died there—
Chorus   Go the fields and hoe.
We starved and toiled by night and day ;
We fought with savages on the way ;
Till we came to this place, where now we say—
Chorus   Go to the fields and hoe.

But our leader, Bula-Matari—
Chorus   Go to the fields and hoe.
Was always so " hodari " (clever)—
Chorus   Go to the fields and hoe.
And our little masters led the way

Through forest, rivers, mire, and clay,
Till we came to this place, where we can say—
Chorus   Go to the fields and hoe.

We came to the open country ;
Chorus   Go to the fields and hoe.
There were cattle and sheep in plenty ;
Chorus   Go to the fields and hoe.
We ate, we drank, we rose to play,
And we laughed and sang like children gay,
When we came to this place, where we could say—
Chorus   Go the fields and hoe.

It was very inspiriting to hear the axes and hoes all come down together in time as the men sang " Go to the fields and hoe."

Frequently large rats, which abounded in great numbers about our fort, would scamper out from hollow trees as the men struck them with their axes, and this was at once a signal for every one to seize sticks and give chase. The rats ran in and out among the men's legs, while they struck wildly everywhere in the greatest excitement, often hitting each other across the shins, shouting and laughing withal like a lot of children. Sometimes a huge poisonous puff adder would glide hissing from under a rotting log, or a brilliant blue and red horned cerastus—a most deadly snake —would drop from the bough of a tree almost on the men's backs. Then there was a stampede, for our men with their bare legs and feet were very much afraid of them, and

"CORNFIELDS ROUND FORT BODO."

would run away shouting to one of us white men, " Hi, Master! here 's a snake, kill him !" Then we would run up and despatch it with our sticks, and the Zanzibaris, after he was dead, chopped him viciously to bits with their hoes, and hurled curses at the whole family of snakes. All these little events created a diversion, and took away somewhat from the monotony of the day's work.

And so, at last, after many days' work, we had cleared quite a large tract of land all round the Fort. It was several acres in extent, and in a few weeks' time we had the satisfaction of seeing green cornfields springing up around us, giving promise of a plentiful harvest.

You must understand that all this time we had to be most vigilant and careful in keeping a good look out for the savage natives who lived in the forest round us. Our men were very foolhardy and often went out in twos and threes and strayed far from the fort in search of ripe bananas or plantains. Often they came in wounded, and several times men went out who never returned, having probably been killed by the savages, who unceasingly prowled about the plantations and lay in wait to kill them. They became so bold that at last we found it necessary to send out a party of ten men as scouts every day to drive away any natives they might find lurking near the plantations and fields.

Whilst we were at the fort we constantly came upon traces of the dwarfs, who, as I said before, abounded in the neighbourhood. They were most artful and cunning in sticking poisoned spikes in the paths in order to lame our men, and in laying in wait for them in the bushes. There must have been several thousands of these dangerous little people in the forest around us.

Far away back in the forest we had come upon little temporary encampments made of boughs of trees and green leaves. In these we found tiny bows and arrows, little spears and diminutive-looking pots. We could not think what sort of people these could be who inhabited these queer little huts and used such tiny weapons. At last, after passing a good many of these settlements, some of our scouts suddenly came upon a small band of dwarfs, busily engaged in peeling bananas in the midst of the forest. Our men pounced on them and captured two, a man and a woman. Mr. Stanley christened them Adam and Eve. They were brought before us in fear and trembling, for to them we must have looked like giants, and they evidently thought we were going to eat them. We tried to reassure them and made gentle crooning noises over them. We put some beads into their hands and closed their little fingers over them—for they were too frightened to shut them themselves—but there

MR. STANLEY CHRISTENED THEM ADAM AND EVE.

they stood, shivering and shaking before us, with the beads dribbling out of their fingers and their little knees knocking together from sheer terror. However, after a while we managed to calm their fears. We smiled sweetly at the little man and chucked the little woman under the chin, and so by degrees they felt rather less uncomfortable, and at last became *quite* certain that we did not want to eat them.

Then we began to talk to them by signs and gestures, using the few words which we knew of their language, asking them who they were, and information about the country in general.

Now, I must tell you there are certain tribes in Africa who talk in dialects resembling the Swahili—which is the language of Zanzibar. Many of the common words, such as corn, water, etc., are very similar in this group of dialects. Some of our Negroes, who had frequently travelled in different countries with Arab caravans, had picked up a number of words which were used by the natives in the forest. These words they eked out with a great many expressive gestures, by which means they were able to converse tolerably easily with the natives of the forest. For instance, we wanted to know whether there were bananas in the country ahead of us. Well, a Zanzibari took up a banana from the ground, and holding it up before the little people, pointed a-head, and asked by signs if there was anything like it in the country ahead of us. The dwarfs understood at once and smilingly held up their left arms, and placing their right hands upon their forearms, they grunted expressively; meaning to say there were bananas as big as their forearms. Our interpreter then asked them with most telling gestures if there were plenty. " Ugh ! Ugh ! Ugh !" grunted the dwarfs, delightedly, holding their hands about a foot in front of their little stomachs, by which they meant to say that bananas were so plentiful in the country ahead that our stomachs would be swelled to that size from the quantities we should be able to eat.

Of course we were able to understand such gestures perfectly, and so we were able to converse quite freely with the pigmies.

These pigmies are generally believed to represent the original people who inhabited the forest which extended over the whole of Equatorial Africa. Other larger tribes have grown up and have scattered the pigmies, so that they no longer have the forest all to themselves.

Several travellers have spoken of them, but they only saw them in such small numbers that it was usually supposed they did not represent any distinct nation. We now, however, struck right through a country peopled by several thousands of dwarfs.

The dwarfs seldom have fixed villages, but roam about the forest in small bands, usually consisting of members of one family, and they are never known of their own free will to leave the forest for the open country.

They live solely on the produce of the chase, and form small temporary encampments near to the villages and clearings of the larger forest natives. With these they exchange the spoils of their hunting expeditions, such as meat, skins, feathers, etc., for corn, bananas, or such things as they require. They are very clever in setting traps and snares for the small animals which abound in the forest, and in digging pitfalls, which they artfully cover with boughs and leaves in order to catch the elephants, who, thinking it is solid ground, walk over the boughs and tumble through into the pits, while the dwarfs, who have been watching in the trees close by, jump down and kill them with their spears. When they have killed an elephant they build little huts all round and remain there until they have eaten him entirely up. We often came upon an old pitfall with the remains of little huts all round it, and the elephant bones lying about on the ground.

The dwarfs are the most primitive people it is possible to imagine, in fact, they may be called the gipsies of the forest.

They are cannibals, and in some cases have their teeth

filed—in order—so we were told—to eat human flesh with greater facility. You know, children, when you are fighting these dwarfs it is rather humiliating to feel that they look upon you, not so much as a human being, but rather as an appetising meal. Of our party I was always the least thin, and my fellow officers used to chaff me and say that the pigmies looked at me with hungry eyes, and their mouths watered to think what a splendid steak they could cut off me if they could only get me! But I am thankful to say they never did ! When any of their own people die they always eat them, unless the person dies of a skin disease.

The pigmies are fierce, brave, and cunning ; their tiny bows, poisoned arrows, and barbed spears making them very formidable assailants. You can easily understand, therefore, that the larger natives are generally afraid to offend them, for they are quick to resent any slight put upon them, and, like most little people, are very spiteful.

Their settlements are sometimes formed of several dozens of little huts, about three feet six inches high and three feet in diameter, which are made of boughs and green leaves.

We were told that in some parts of the forest the pigmies sleep with their bodies in the huts and their legs sticking out of the doors. Over their entire bodies they have a thick fell of stiff greyish hair, which gives them a dusty and peculiarly elfish appearance. They have, moreover, a strong and most unpleasant odour, like the lions' cage at the Zoological Gardens—our Zanzibaris said it was because they ate human flesh.

I remember a little dwarf woman in Emin Pasha's country. Emin was measuring her height and size, and asked me to help him. The little woman was dreadfully frightened, for she thought we were going to kill her, and she broke out into a cold perspiration from sheer terror. The smell she emitted from her skin was so strong that I had to wash my hands several times after touching her before I could get rid of the unpleasant odour. The dwarfs usually measure about four feet ten inches in height, but they are well formed and exceedingly intelligent. They have a language of their own, but ordinarily speak the language of the natives in whose country they are staying. The dwarf babies are very funny! They are like tadpoles, all head and stomach, and looking so round, fat, and shiny, are most tempting to smack. They run about and play together in the forest, and almost as soon as they can walk they begin to practise shooting with tiny bows and arrows.

Emin had a little dwarf boy, and I asked him one day

to show me how he could shoot. He answered, "Speak, Master, what shall I shoot at ?"

I pointed out to him a cock which was in the act of crowing at some little distance. The boy smiled disdain-fully at the easiness of the task, and quickly drawing the string of his bow, he transfixed the bird through the head.

Now, from what I have told you, you must not think these dwarfs are of a low type of humanity. You will make a great mistake if you think that.

I will tell you about a little dwarf woman who was the Queen of the Pigmies.

She was captured in a fight, and remained in our camp for a long time, and every one became fond of her, for she was so cheerful and bright and industrious, and was full of fun and laughter. It is true that when she came to us first her only clothing was an iron girdle and a necklace of dog's teeth over her little brown skin, and very nice she looked in it, just like a little bronze statue, and she was modest and well behaved too.

She took a great fancy to our doctor, and used to cook his food and bring him fire for his pipe. After a while the nights became so cold that Dr. Parke wished to give her some clothes. We were all so poverty-stricken that we had not much to give her, but he gave her what he could, which was an old Macintosh coat—once upon a time it was

"SOMETIMES I WOULD LEND HER MY LOOKING GLASS."

"I CAN SEE HER NOW WALKING PROUDLY THROUGH THE CAMP."

waterproof, but it had lost its waterproof qualities long since. Though she had never worn clothes before the little dwarf dame took most kindly to it, and I can see her now, walking proudly through the camp, with the Macintosh coat trailing on the ground. She would twist her head this way and that to get a good view of the sweep of her garment behind, with the same gestures and evident pleasure with which a lady in a London drawing room would manage her train of six feet long.

She would look with pity upon the other women in the camp, who were not to her mind dressed as elegantly as herself. She would contemplate the noble sweep of her garment with childlike pleasure, I will not say with pride, for a good heart is never proud, and even the joy of possessing such a magnificent garment as that old Macintosh coat could not spoil the kind heart of that sweet, simple-natured little dwarf dame.

Sometimes as a treat I would lend her my looking glass, before which—if I allowed it, she would sit for hours gazing at her face with a pleased smile.

Now most of you have seen a lady when she comes into a room where there is a mirror and thinks no one is looking. She will go before the looking glass and give her tucker a twitch on one side and fluff her hair up rapidly and lightly with her hands, and then, with a side look into the mirror, she will tilt up her chin, give herself one more finishing touch, and turning round will be ready to face the whole world.

Well, I have often seen that little dwarf lady go through just such movements as that before my looking glass. She would give her necklace of dog's teeth a hitch to the right, and would fluff up her black wool more fetchingly over her little ears ; and then, turning round, she would receive the advances of some love-sick Zanzibari swain with all the airs of a great lady—and she had a great many admirers, for she was very good looking.

And so, I say, do not think these pigmies are a low caste people. I have travelled through many countries and have seen strange people, but the more I travel, the more the conviction grows upon me, that big or small, black or white, women are much the same all the world over, and even though they have never seen them before, they all love pretty frocks !

For many months that little pigmy dame accompanied our caravan, endearing herself to all by her bright, cheer-ful, kindly ways. Alas ! in the open country, the con-tinuous marching and the heat of the sun were too much for her, after being accustomed to the dark shades of the forest all her life. And so she sickened and pined for her forest home, and when we were only twenty days' march from the coast we were obliged to leave her behind with a friendly tribe of natives who promised to look after her.

We were all sorry to part with that gentle little lady, for we felt that some of the sunlight had gone from the camp, and in those days we needed some cheering and softening element in our midst.

We know not now what has become of her, she may be still living with the natives, or she may be dead : but she has left behind her the feeling with us that in the hearts of rough untutored " savages " the same kindly human element beats strongly as in ours, making us all kin.

And now I have come to the end of the chapter, and hope I have been able to interest you children. If so, in the next chapter I will tell you some more about ourselves and our life.

CHAPTER II.

THE STORY OF MAHOMET.

 WILL now draw you a little picture of Fort Bodo, in which we were destined to spend so many months. In the inner part of the Fort were the mud-houses of Mr. Stanley and ourselves, a store house, and three houses for some of our chiefs. In the middle were two large granaries for Indian corn. These were raised upon legs nine feet high, in order to keep out the rats, which infested the place. Outside, in another inclosure, were two long lines of huts for the Zanzibaris, behind which were their little gardens for growing native vegetables or tobacco.

The whole place was kept beautifully clean and neat, for in those hot countries any dirt or garbage lying about immediately brings fever and sickness. Therefore, every day when work was finished we had the whole place swept clean, and large fires were kept burning, into which the refuse was thrown—a kind of Gehenna.

We had quite a number of animals with us which gave the place a homelike appearance.

There were four cows that we had brought back with us

"THE LITTLE ZANZIBAR BOYS DELIGHTED IN MAKING THE TWO FIGHT."

from the open country near the Albert Nyanza ; we also had twelve goats, several of which had kids, and large numbers of chickens. These animals were very tame, and used to wander about the fort. It was pleasant to watch the chickens clucking and scratching about, while the kids leaped and played together round their mothers. These homelike scenes were soothing in the middle of that wild forest, and we loved to hear the well-known sounds : the lowing of cows, the bleating of goats, the crowing of cocks, and the chuckling of a hen as she announced proudly to all the world that she had laid an egg. Amongst our pets we had a tame heron, which used to hop about the fort picking up snails and slugs. It was amusing to see the rivalry between this bird and Mr. Stanley's fox terrier Randy. Whenever the heron approached Mr. Stanley's house Randy would dash out and drive it away, barking furiously. The heron, which was lame in one leg, hopped about in the most comical way, and made vicious pecks at Randy, who never dared to approach too close to the bird, having several times experienced the sharpness of its beak. The little Zanzibar boys delighted in making the two fight, and would dance round clapping their hands and encouraging them.

To many of you children, who see such scenes every day, these things would pass unnoticed. But to us men, who for so many months had been accustomed to fight with savages and cannibals, and had lived through wild and weird experiences, these simple scenes came as a relief, and were a rest to minds wearied and hardened from long struggling with death and disaster. They were as a breath from home, and brought with them a calm and civilizing influence, which, God knows, is necessary to men amid such rough surroundings. You children, who can get anything you want from shops, cannot understand what pleasure we took in all the little things we made for ourselves. I remember, when our house was built, I made a table of which I was extremely proud. I had no tools to make it with, except a hammer and an old cold chisel. Near the fort I found a rough native-made plank, and at this I chipped and chipped during my spare time. After I had brought it to a certain rough smoothness, I fixed four rather shaky and uneven legs to it, and planting it proudly in the middle of the floor of our hut, said to my fellow officers, " There, boys, we've got a real table at last."

Well, that table was warranted to upset anything that was put upon it! Some of my fellow officers would incautiously put down their cups of tea on it, and I can almost hear them still exclaiming, " confound that old table of Jephson's! There it is again, all my tea upset!"

However, in spite of it all, I used to walk round that table and view it from different points of vantage with a feeling of intense pride. No shop-made English table from Maple's or Hampton's could ever be so beautiful to me as was that ricketty plank in our little mud hut in Africa.

Then we made bedsteads, too, and put them in the four corners of our huts. Dear me! We have reason to remember those bedsteads, they were as uneven as a switch-back railway. Still, we were lenient to their short-comings, and covered their inequalities with a plentiful sprinkling of dry leaves, and bore patiently with all their deficiencies, simply because we had made them ourselves.

It was just the same out of doors—never did cornfields look to us so lovely; never was there, in our eyes, a crop so fine, or corn so sweet and succulent as that which came from the fields which we ourselves had planted.

And so, my young friends, hard work honestly and conscientiously done always carries with it a certain reward, a proud feeling that you have done some real good yourself. Who among you does not know how sweet the vegetables taste grown in the little patch of ground which your mother or father has given you in the garden? With what pride you eat the little bunch of radishes, the first fruits of your labours!

Well, so it was with us men. All the fresh and natural feelings we had as children came back to us in the midst of that dark forest, and prevented our becoming callous and hardened.

Sunday at the Fort was always a day of rest, and was eagerly looked forward to by Europeans and Zanzibaris alike, for we could always lie in bed and rest till breakfast time, and could do many little things for which we had no time during the week.

Early in the morning our men used to troop down to the creek close by to bathe, and wash such poor clothes as they had—for the Negro is, by nature, a cleanly being, and does not love dirt and disorder; then they would sit under the trees chatting and smoking as they waited for their clothes to dry, which had been spread out in the sun upon the bushes, for in those days they were poor and had only the clothes they stood in.

Some of our men, however, were great " Mally-Daddies " (Zanzibar word for dandies), and after washing themselves and fluffing out their wool, they would arrange their scanty clothes to the best advantage, and taking a little stick in their hands, strutted about the fort just as they were accustomed to do in the town of Zanzibar.

Others might be seen preparing bananas, beans, yams, corn, or such wild herbs as they had collected about the clearings; and groups of them gathered about the fires, talking and laughing quietly, as they stirred or tasted the simmering contents of the pots, and discussed the important question as to whether more " pili-pili " (pepper) would be an improvement or not.

The very goats and cattle seemed to know it was

Sunday, and lay lazily chewing the cud and blinking in the sun ; while the chickens, making little gentle clucking sounds, plumed themselves or dusted their feathers in the hollows they had scratched under the shade of the granaries.

The whole place had that air of quiet and repose which seems only to exist on Sunday.

On these mornings Mr. Stanley generally sat in his house and wrote up the rough notes he had made during the week. We officers took the opportunity of mending our tattered clothes and making rough boots (for those we brought from Europe had long since worn out, and for many months we wore only such boots as we were able to make for ourselves. It was difficult work at first, but we soon became great adepts in the art of shoemaking.

We made the upper part of our boots of raw, sun-dried cowhide, the soles were made from seasoned buffalo hide which we found in the native huts. In the open country we found numbers of hide shields which the natives wore round their bodies to protect them from arrows. They cut large oblong pieces of thick buffalo hide, and these they hang up in the roofs of their huts, and in a few months' time the heat and smoke of the fires season the hide and make it hard and impervious to arrows. When the hide is sufficiently cured the natives bend it into a cylindrical shape and lace it up round their bodies. These hardened shields made excellent leather for boot soles, and we brought quite a number of them with us to the fort for that purpose. We manufactured awls out of sharpened nails and fixed them in wooden handles ; with these we made holes in the hide for the thread to pass through. Big needles were very precious in those days, and were always jealously guarded by us. I made an excellent needle by filing the knob off the end of an old brass bodkin which was in my housewife. How useful that old needle was ! I have got it still, as a momento of our shoemaking days. On one side of it is stamped " Victoria, Queen of England, born 1819," and, on the other side " Ascended the throne 1837."

It is, however, so worn from constant use that I can only just decipher the inscription. If only that old needle could speak, what tales it could tell! It has travelled over many thousand miles of rough country, it has sewn more ragged clothes, I suppose, than any other needle existing, and it certainly has helped to manufacture the strangest looking of shoes. It has pricked the thorns from many a lame and weary foot, and my European and Zanzibari friends in the expedition knew well its value. And it now lies before me. It is true its eye is sadly worn out of shape, its body is dull, its nose is bent and blunted, but still that old brass needle is more beautiful to me than the finest needle made of the brightest and newest steel ; for it is an old and tried friend, and has saved my feet from many a blister and many a sore in that long and weary march through Central Africa.

And so the morning would pass peacefully and usefully away, and after our midday meal was over Mr. Stanley and we officers, taking our chairs, used to go up the path to the edge of the cornfields and sit smoking our pipes on a little mound under the shadow of a great tree, whose branches threw a cool and chequered shade over the broad pathway. From here we could see the fort and the waving green cornfields around it ; fields which were the work of our own hands. We used to talk of our work, our plans and experiences ; of the time when we should reach Emin Pasha and be able to help him ; of the Rear Column and our companions far away, and finally, of our people and home. The breeze rustling the leaves of the trees carried the sounds of the fort faintly to our ears, and in the distance we could hear our men singing verses of the Khoran in the monotonous voice peculiar to Mahome-dans.

As the afternoon shadows lengthened our Zanzibaris would stroll out in twos and threes, and join us under the tree until most of our people were gathered round us.

After some talk Raschid, our head chief, would ask Mr. Stanley for a story, and he, ever ready to gossip with the men, would tell them some story from the Old Testament, or of Aladdin and the Wonderful Lamp. Various comments and interruptions came from the men as they listened to the stories and asked questions on various points they did not quite understand. They seemed best to like Scriptural tales, which, they said, reminded them of their own Mahomedan stories.

I remember one afternoon as we sat together saying, " Raschid, I have seen you writing verses of the Khoran with a charred stick on boards, and the men sit in front of the boards and sing what they say is written on them. Now, do they understand what they are singing, do they really know anything about Mahomet ? "

" Yea, Master, verily they do," answered Raschid. " All of us know about Him ; even Binza there, who was only a Ma-shenzi (Pagan) two years ago, have we not taught him the beliefs of Islam ? Speak, boy, and tell the little Master what you know of the prophet."

" Yes, speak up boy," said all the men, " tell the Masters the story of Mahomet."

Binza, smiling shyly, rose to his feet and shifting uneasily from leg to leg began to tell the story in the picturesque language of Zanzibar.

"Master, it is true M'seh Raschid has told me of the Prophet, still, I am but a thoughtless boy, and it may be that I have forgotten part of the story, for, as you know, we black boys. think more of filling our stomachs and of sleeping than of anything else.   But I will tell you as well as I can remember all that he told me.

" Far, far away, towards the rising sun, is a country called Arabia.   It is a land of sand and rocks, where the sun beats down like a fire at midday, and makes the whole land quiver and swim before the eyes.   In this country is a town called Muscat, it is the same same town, Master, from which the grandfather of our Said (Sultan) of Zanzibar originally came, and brought with him the Maho-medan religion, which, as you know, is now the religion of all Zanzibaris.

" Long, long ago, so long that I cannot tell you the number of years, there lived a man called Mahomet—to whom we bow.   He was a man of good family, and used to drive His uncle's camels with merchandise between Muscat and Jerusalem.

" Being very clever, and of an inquiring mind, He used, while staying in these places, to spend all His spare time with the holy men who lived in caves near by, and among the hermits in the country round His native town of Muscat.   From these holy men He obtained books, which

He used diligently to read during His journeys between Jerusalem and Muscat. From leading this life He became well versed in the Scriptures and in all Holy Lore, and grew to be fanatical in His love of all holy things.

" One night as He was sleeping on the roof of His house at Muscat, the Angel Gabriel appeared to Him, and told Him he had come to call Him into the presence of God, who had a great work for Him to do.

" The angel then transported Mahomet to the Holy Hill of Jerusalem in two hours, which to ordinary mortals was seven days' journey from Muscat.

" He here gave Him a steed called El Borak, upon whose back He was able to ascend in the space of a few minutes into the Seventh Heaven, in which God dwelt. To an ordinary mortal it was a journey of three thousand five hundred years, but God was pleased to permit His servant and prophet Mahomet—in whom we trust—to reach His Presence immediately. On reaching the First Heaven He saw the prophet Moses ; in the Second Heaven was the prophet Joseph ; in the Third Heaven was the prophet Jacob ; in the Fourth Heaven was the prophet Isaac ; and in the Fifth Heaven was the prophet Abraham ; and in the Sixth Heaven He bowed before the prophet Jesus, who was sent down to conduct Him to the Seventh Heaven, into the Presence of God.

" He prostrated Himself before the Divine Presence, and God told Him He had a great work for Him to do. He was to found a New Religion among God's chosen people, and it was to be called Islam. After explaining to Mahomet the beliefs and laws of this New Religion God laid a strict injunction upon Him that the people were to pray fifty times a day.

" Having heard all God's commands, He again mounted the steed El Borak, who immediately began to descend.

" On reaching the First Heaven He told the prophet Moses all that God had commanded Him to do, and the strict injunction that the people should pray fifty times a day.

" And Moses said, ' Your people are wicked and slothful people, given up to pleasure and lust, they will never pray fifty times a day, you will gain no converts to your New Religion, turn again into the Presence of God and entreat Him to lessen the number.'

" Mahomet, therefore, returned to the Seventh Heaven, and prostrating Himself, entreated God to lessen the number to forty times, then to thirty, and so on until he had reduced the number to five times. And God said five times was the law, and the law must be kept.

" The Prophet—to whom our greetings—then descended to the Holy Hill of Jerusalem, and the Angel Gabriel transported Him back to Muscat. In the morning, when

He awakened from His sleep, He pondered over all that had passed, and went out in the wilderness for forty days and forty nights, and was lost in deep meditation and prayer.

" And after these days had elapsed He went out among the people and preached the New Religion called Islam, which rapidly spread among the nations of the earth.

" And this, Master," said Binza, " is the story of the Prophet before whom we bow—as I remember it, but it may be that I have not told it right. Speak, Father Raschid, and tell the Masters if I have said truly."

" Yes, boy, you have spoken the truth," said Raschid. " Among the Arabs there is but one belief."

" Eh Baba ! " exclaimed Murabo, " is it not true that our Said of Zanzibar, Prince Burghash, believes it to be impossible for the Prophet to have been transported into the Seventh Heaven so rapidly ? I think, M'seh (old man), you are wrong."

" Nonsense," answered Raschid, with an air of dignity. " In these days young men think that they know better than their elders, but things were different when I was young. *We* used gratefully to listen to what our elders told us. Ah, the world is sadly changed ; the young men now wish to take the places of the elders—there is no place for old men in these days ! "

" Nay, M'seh, he meant no harm," exclaimed the rest of the men, " we all know that you are our father and mother."

But Raschid's dignity was hurt, and shaking the dust from his feet, he left the group, repeating that there was no place for old men in these days.

But now the shadows had grown long and the daylight was closing in. We reluctantly broke up the group and returned to the fort, agreeing that every Sunday we would meet under the tree and tell stories.

And so night fell on the Peaceful Fort, and we sat down to our frugal suppers, refreshed by our Sunday rest, and ready with the daylight to begin the work of a new week.

CHAPTER III.

 FIND under the date of April 1st, 1888, the following remark in my journal :

" All this (Sunday) morning we have been trying our hands at soap making, and by mid-day managed to make quite a decent amount, and are all very proud of the result."

For months we had been without soap, and the only way we had of washing our clothes at all was to boil them in a big native-made earthenware jar. We only had the clothes we stood in, so that while our servants were boiling them we had to wrap ourselves in blankets and sit in our huts or tents until they were ready for us to put on again.

The night before, being Saturday night, a cow had been killed and the meat divided among the men as a treat for their Sunday dinner. We had taken most of the fat, and with it proposed to make soap. We were novices in the art of soap-making, but, as you all know, "necessity is the mother of invention," and so we invented as we went on. Fat or oil, we knew, was the chief ingredient, and that the next thing was to obtain potash and soda. We cudgelled our brains as to how we could obtain soda. We had observed that when we burnt a certain kind of tree it yielded a very white ash, so we mixed this with water and used it as a wash for whitewashing the walls of our mud houses. Well, one thing led to another. One morning some of us noticed that if this whitewash was left standing all night the ash sank to the bottom, leaving the water a clear yellowish colour. This water had an acrid, bitter taste, which we knew must contain a certain amount of soda, and so, by a mere chance we discovered this method of making soap.

To return to my story. On this particular Sunday morning we collected all the fat, mixed it with a quantity of the ash-water, and pouring it all into the largest pot we could find, set it on a big fire to boil. We were all much interested in the experiment, and every now and again went out to see that the boys were keeping up the fire and stirring the pot.

From early morning till midday we kept it going, and at last had the satisfaction of seeing the mixture gradually thickening and becoming like soap.

When we considered that it had boiled enough we let it cool and made the thick brown mass into balls about the size of an orange. It had not the delicate odour of Pears' soap, but what a triumph it was to find that on using it it lathered splendidly! With what satisfaction we contemplated that row of dirty-looking brown balls, and what pride we experienced in feeling that we had actually been able, in that lonely forest, to make real soap! The Zanzibaris were all equally interested in watching our soap-making, and were proud that their white masters should be so clever. As we gathered under the tree that afternoon they all talked about it and wondered how we, who in our own country had been accustomed to have everything we wanted, should be willing to come into Africa, where we had to do things ourselves and "work like slaves."

"Ah!" said Uledi, "though the Masters are accustomed in Uliah (Europe) to do nothing but eat and sleep, it is trouble which has taught them how to work with their hands. And hunger, too, how it teaches people! Do you remember the starvation days before we came to this place, and what they taught us? Our little Masters were proud, Allah! how proud! when we started, but hunger and trouble has brought us all together. In those days, white men or black, we were all in the same pit, and but

for those times, perhaps, we should not now understand
our little Masters, or they us."

"Eh, Wallah! but hunger bends the stiff neck and
softens the heart. Tell the Master, Murabo, for you are a
"fundi" (skilled hand) at story-telling, tell them the story
we tell our children in Zanzibar of the Lion and Mr.
Hunger."

Then Murabo, who was the wit of the party, and always
full of saws and sayings, got up and told us the following
tale.

"Once upon a time, in the desert of M'Gunda Makali,
which lies far to the East, in the country of Unyamwezi,
there lived a Lion. He was the terror of all the country,
being the strongest and fiercest lion in the whole of Africa.
When he roared it was as if the thunder shook the earth,
and the beasts of the forest bowed down before him, for he
was the king of them all.

"The elephant and rhinoceros, the leopard, buffalo, and
hyena, all owned him as their chief, and did his bidding in
obedience and fear. He dwelt in a dark cave under the
shadow of a great rock, which was strewn all round with the
skulls and bones of his enemies, who had come from time
to time to try their strength against him.

"Allah! Master, he was a fearsome beast! As he stood
before his cave tossing his tawny mane, gnashing those

terrible teeth, and lashing his tail, he was a sight to make the bravest quake! And at night, when from afar his fearful roar boomed across the country and echoed among the rocks, the prowling hyena would slink away in fear and trembling, and the antelope would spring from his mossy couch by the running stream, and speed, terror-stricken, across the plain.

"The young warrior princes of Uganda and Unyoro, of Usukuma and Kuanda had all come to do battle with the Lion, for his fame had gone through all the land. The African bards sang of his wondrous strength, and of the bloody battles which had been fought at the mouth of that dark cave in the gloomy wilderness of M'Gunda Makali. But one after another the Lion had killed them all, and his cave had become a charnel house, strewn with the bones of his enemies.

"And so every one who came against him fell before him, till at last he cried out in the pride of his heart, 'I am the chief of all the land, for no one is so strong and great as I.'

"Now hard by the Lion's den there dwelt a rabbit. He was in no way afraid of his savage neighbour, for he was so small and weak that he was beneath the lion's enmity, and was, therefore, treated with a certain tolerance by him.

"You know how it is, Master. Look at big Musa there, he is strong enough to fell a buffalo, and no man dare

quarrel with him. Yet you have seen how the children in
the camp play tricks upon him, and tease and worry him
like mosquitoes, for they know they are so small that he
will never hurt them.

"Well, so it was with the Rabbit and the Lion."

Murabo here ducked his head, as a corn cob, thrown by
the subject of his remarks, whizzed past his ear, and the
"big Musa," with a broad grin on his good-natured face,
lazily re-settled himself against the trunk of a tree.

"Well, one morning when the Rabbit was out for a walk,
he met the Lion.

"'Good day, B'wana Lion,' squeaked the Rabbit.

"'Good mor-r-r-ning, Rabbit,' roared the Lion. 'Look
at me, did you ever see any one so great and strong as I?'

"And the Lion, making the dust fly as he pawed the
ground, gave out such a terrific roar that the Rabbit, nearly
deafened, put his paws to his ears.

"'Thou art great, it is true, B'wana Lion,' answered the
Rabbit, 'yet I know a man who is even stronger than
thou.'

"'Ugh! Ugh! Ugh! Where is he? What is his name?
Show him to me. Let me tear him in pieces and grind his
bones to powder.' And the Lion struck the ground
furiously with his huge paws and made the whole country
side ring with his deafening roar.

"'His name is B'wana Hunger,' replied the Rabbit, 'and he is everywhere. If thou wilt wait till to-morrow, I will lead thee to a place where thou wilt be able to find him.'

"'It is well,' yelled the Lion, beside himself with rage.

'Only show him to me to-morrow, and we will see who is the stronger.'

"'Verily, we will see,' muttered the Rabbit to himself, as he bade the Lion good morning.

" All that day the Lion could be heard roaring in his cave, as he prepared for the next day's encounter with his unknown enemy, B'wana Hunger.

" The beasts of the forest heard the thunder from afar, and wondered in fear and trembling what it could mean.

" Meanwhile the Rabbit went gaily off to his warren, and calling all his friends and relations round him, unfolded his plans.

" ' Now, friends, I have a plan in my head, and I want you all to help me to carry it out.   You hear that roaring away in the distance, and you all know it is our dreaded neighbour, the bloodthirsty Lion, who is the scourge and terror of the whole countryside.   Now I have an idea in my brain,' said the Rabbit, meditatively scratching his head, ' by which we, the smallest and feeblest of all the animals, can rid the land of this scourge and free the country from this tyrant.

" ' I have this morning seen B'wana Lion, and I have told him that I know a man called B'wana Hunger, who is stronger than he.   I have promised to show him to B'wana Lion to-morrow.   Now, I want your help, and you must all do as I tell you and be guided by me.   Will you help me ? '

" ' We will, we swear it,' cried all the rabbits together. ' Only show us how.'

"'Thank you,' answered the Rabbit, 'I knew I could depend upon you.'

"'Now brother Sandy, take with you fifteen of your brothers, with their axes, and go to the forest and cut down a number of strong young saplings.'

"'You, brother Brindle, take thirty or forty of your friends, and bring the saplings to the wooded dell near the river. Meanwhile Long-Whisker and I will take the rest with spades, and cut a deep trench in which to plant the poles as you bring them.'

"'Queri!' cried they all, and away scampered the rabbits to perform their various tasks. All day long they worked hard without any rest, and by nightfall they had made a strong inclosure with no outlet but a narrow gate.

"That night they went to bed well pleased with their labours, certain that their plan would be successful. Early next morning the Rabbit was at the appointed place, where he found the Lion eager for his encounter with Mr. Hunger.

"'Good morning, B'wana Lion,' sweetly squeaked the Rabbit, 'Are you ready for your fight with Mr. Hunger?'

"'Ready!' roared the Lion 'I've been thinking of nothing else all night. Where is he? Show him to me without delay,' and the Lion ground his teeth in a frenzy of expectation and rage.

"'Follow me,' said the Rabbit, 'he is not far off.'

"The Lion, still growling in a threatening manner, followed the Rabbit, who led him to the entrance of the inclosure he had built the day before.

"'He's in there, waiting for you,' said the Rabbit, pointing through the gateway.

"With a mighty bound the Lion leapt through the entrance, and the Rabbit immediately closed the gate after him.

"The Lion rapidly searched the inclosure, and asked with a defiant roar, 'Where is Mr. Hunger?'

"'He will come soon enough, only wait a little,' said the Rabbit, as he turned on his heel and rejoined his companions.

"The Lion waited and waited, and made several attempts to get out of the trap, but the cunning rabbits had made it so strong and high that he was forced to remain where he was.

"After two days the Rabbit returned. 'How are you, Mr. Lion?' asked he, as he looked through the bars. 'Have you seen any signs of Mr. Hunger yet?'

"'Not yet,' feebly roared the Lion, 'but I am ready for him when he comes. Only bring him quickly that I may tear him limb from limb.'

"'He will be here shortly now,' said the Rabbit, 'I do not think he will be long,' and he trotted away through the bushes.

"Two more days passed before the Rabbit returned. This time he found the Lion helplessly stretched upon the ground. His skin hung in folds over his ribs, and the head he had once held so proudly aloft was now sunk between his paws in the dust.

"'Have you encountered Mr. Hunger yet?' inquired the Rabbit.

"'Oh! Oh! Oh!' moaned the Lion, 'what is this strange faintness which has come over me, blinding my eyes and sapping my strength? It is something that I have never felt before, for it has taken away my strength and humbled me to the dust.'

" 'Ah!' said the Rabbit triumphantly, ' it is Mr. Hunger, I told you he would come, and that he was stronger even than you.'

" The Lion looked reproachfully at the Rabbit ; he made one more effort to rise, but rolling helplessly over on the sand, he breathed his last.

" Quickly the news went through the land that the Lion was dead. The beasts of the forest soon gathered round the body of their dead king, and asked in astonishment who was the enemy who had slain him; and the rabbits answered that it was Mr. Hunger.

" And so you see," concluded Murabo, " what hunger can do. It tames the fiercest of us, and makes our hearts like water. We, Master of all people, know what it can do, and how sometimes it makes the kindest of us selfish and cruel."

" But observe, boys," interrupted Raschid, who was always ready to point a moral to every tale, " the Lion was so pleased with his strength and his head became so swollen with pride, that he boasted that no one was so strong as he. Therefore, do not forget young men, that though you may be as strong as lions, and swift as ante-lopes to-day, do not boast, for a time may come when

hunger and sickness will drag you down, even as Mr. Hunger humbled the proud Lion in the dust."

"What you say, Raschid, is quite true," broke in Binza, "but though the Lion may have been proud and cruel, I have no opinion whatever of the Rabbit, who deceived the Lion when he trusted him. He had two faces, and his heart was no bigger than a pebble. For my part, I think the Rabbit deserved to starve, and the beasts of the forest should have torn him to pieces."

"Allah! listen to Binza," interrupted Saleh, Mr. Stanley's black boy. "He speaks like the Pagan he is, who has only just begun to learn about the Prophet, and is not a true son of Islam. Of course the Rabbit was right, he was the more 'hodari' of the two, for though he was so small he was clever, and outdid the Lion, with all his strength."

"Pagan or not, Saleh," cried Binza furiously, "I had rather be a Pagan and single-hearted than a son of Islam and two-tongued, like the snake that you are. We all know who it is makes so much trouble in the camp, and whispers stories in the B'wana M'Kubwa's ears about us all. You are like the Rabbit, who betrayed the Lion who trusted him, in order to gain credit for being 'hodari' among the beasts of the forest. Bah! let me remain a Pagan then, if that is what Islam puts into your heart."

Saleh, with a gesture of contempt, appealed to us, saying,

E

"Hear, Little Masters, the words of Binza, who a few years ago was not only a Pagan, but a cannibal."

This last taunt cut Binza to the quick, for he always studiously ignored his cannibal descent, and any allusion to it made him beside himself. Starting furiously to his feet, he seized a stick with which to break Saleh's head, and a row seemed imminent.

The men who had been silent and amused spectators of the war of words between the two boys, rose at this juncture to interfere, when suddenly the distant sound of a horn fell upon our ears, and announced the return of a party of scouts, who had been sent out three days before to find a path to the river Ihuru. We therefore broke up the gathering quickly and returned to the Fort, to hear what news they had brought.

CHAPTER IV.

NOTHER Sunday came round, and with it the usual homelike occupations and cares.

Stairs had gone back to Ipoto to fetch the boat, which we had been obliged to leave behind.

All of us missed him about the Fort, for there were so few of us that the absence of one even of our fellow officers made a great gap in our little family circle. Besides, too, we all liked him well, he was Mr. Stanley's second in command, and we found it pleasant to work with him. He had left one of his servants, Abedi, behind in my care, as the boy was unwell and unable to march rapidly. He was an amusing little fellow and entertained us often with his stories and remarks. He used to tell me about his life in Zanzibar, and about his father, who was a carpenter, and had made him a wonderful bed, which he described in glowing terms; according to him there never was such a bed. He told me about a favourite dog he had, called Pensil, and a dozen other little things, all of which he chattered about as I sat mending my clothes on Sunday mornings.

There were great numbers of black and white wagtails about the Fort. At night they used to roost in the roofs of the houses, and all day long one might hear their cheerful song as they chirped to each other and ran along the ground after insects, wagging their tails and looking so bright and happy. They were as tame as robins, and used sometimes even to come into the houses if they saw some temptingly fat insect near the door.

The Zanzibaris loved to see these wagtails about the huts, and pretended to understand what their different notes signified. Abedi told me if a wagtail came and sang before the door in a particular way, and ran three times round wagging his tail, that it portended the near approach of a friend. And so we whiled away the time until the afternoon ; when we repaired as usual to our tree.

Mr. Stanley used to tell the men the story of Joseph and his brethren, of which they were very fond, and about which they made all sorts of remarks concerning Joseph and his treatment of his brothers. Their interest always grew intense at that part of the story where Joseph sends for Jacob, and Mr. Stanley described in picturesque language the meeting of the young man with his aged father. It was a story which appealed strongly to their sympathies, and tears came into the eyes of many a rough Negro as he listened to the tale; for the Negroes are a natural, simple race, and usually love their old people, looking upon them as a sacred charge, most unlike the young people of the present day, who look upon their old people as a burden and a bore.

When Mr. Stanley had finished the story, Abedi, who had been stroking Randy as he sat by his master's chair, called upon Uledi to tell us the story of how the dog first gave up his wild habits and lived with the children of men.

" Ay, Uledi, tell the Master about it," said Kheri, a huge, good-natured chief, over six feet high, and as black as a coal.

" Nay," said Uledi, " I am no story-teller, and words do not roll from my tongue as they do from Murabo's. He is the best story-teller of us all. Let *him* tell the Masters about it."

" It is always I who am called upon," answered Murabo, "and it is now your turn, Uledi; we all know you have more brains in your head than most of us."

But Uledi was not in a talking mood that day and would only promise that if Murabo would relate the story

of the Dog and the Leopardess he would tell us the story
of Kintu the following Sunday. With this Murabo was
forced to content himself, and getting up began :

"Long years ago, before Zanzibar was a town or the
Arabs had penetrated Africa, the inhabitants lived in their
villages without any domestic animals. There were no
tame cattle, or goats, or even chickens in those days. Any
meat the people required they obtained by hunting the
wild animals of the forest ; game in those days was even
more plentiful than now, so that the natives never wanted
for food, and could kill enough game in a day to last them
a week.

"Now the first wild animal to become tame and domesti-
cated was a dog ; and it fell about thus.

"Far away to the West, near the outskirts of the Great
Forest there dwelt a widowed Leopardess. She lived with
her two cubs, Kenyi and Tomba, in a warm, sandy cave on
the shores of lake Tanganyka. Her husband, some time
before, had fallen into a pitfall and been killed by the
natives, and she now lived alone with her twin cubs, who
were only two months old.

"She was obliged to be out all day long hunting for
food, and was unable to look after her twins, whom she was
forced to leave alone in the cave.

"Like most mothers, she was very fond of her children,

and did not at all like leaving them alone, so at last she determined to engage a nurse.

"She went round the country therefore and told all the beasts of the forest that she wished to find a good, steady nurse who could be depended upon to look after her children carefully. Her friends promised to let it be known that she required a nurse, and on the following day three applicants for the post, a hyena, a fox, and a dog stood before her.

"They asked her what wages she gave, and she told them that they should have a comfortable home in her cave and a share of the meat she brought home at night from her hunting excursions. In return for this the nurse would be required to look after her cubs while she was away.

"'How do you think it would suit you?' asked the Leopardess of the first applicant.

"'He-yah, He-yah! He-yah!' laughed the Hyena. 'I don't know but what it might suit me, if there was not too much to do, He-yah, he-yah, he-yah!' And the Hyena laughed so loud and long that the Leopardess drove him away, saying that such a flighty and flippant creature was not fit to look after *her* precious babies.

"Turning to the second applicant, she said, 'What do you think, Mr. Fox; how would the place suit you?'

"'Well,' said the Fox, 'I don't think the wages are particularly good; but I shall want three evenings out during the week, for I have a family hard by.'

"'Nay,' answered the Leopardess, 'I cannot have my servants running out at night; I know what it means, you will be carrying away all the broken meat and scraps, and I shall have to keep your family as well as yourself. Besides, Mr. Fox, there is a cunning, crafty look in your eyes which I do not like; you too, may go, for I can see that you will not suit me.' And the Leopardess, with a wave of her paw dismissed him.

"'What do you say, Dog?' she then asked.

"'Well, I think, Madam, the place will suit me very well," said the Dog; "all I want is a comfortable home, and I shall be satisfied with the bones; besides, too, I am fond of children.'

"'Very well,' said the Leopardess, 'I think you will suit me exactly; you shall have as many bones as you like. But before engaging you I must make one condition, which is that everything that you eat must be eaten *inside* the cave. If you take anything outside something dreadful will happen, and a terrible disaster will come on me and my family. Do you hear, Dog?' and the Leopardess looked dreadfully savage.

"'I hear, Madam, I quite understand,' humbly answered

the Dog, as he wagged his tail in a deprecating manner. 'It is an easy condition to observe, and I will see that it is fulfilled.'

"'Very well,' said the Leopardess, somewhat mollified by the Dog's humble answer, 'you may consider yourself engaged.'

"For a week all went well. The Dog attended assiduously to his duties; he washed the Leopard cubs, and tended them carefully : he smoothed the sandy floor of the cave, and kept things neat and tidy. When the Leopardess returned each evening tired out after her hunting excursions she found everything in order; the cubs were clean and neat, and when she lay down each night and called for the twins to suckle them, the Dog brought them and laid them by her side. Everything was as it should be, and she felt thankful to have engaged so good and trusty a servant. So things went on smoothly, until one evening the Leopardess returned from a very successful hunting excursion, bringing with her the meat of a beautiful fat giraffe.

"Oh! those marrowbones! How the Dog smacked his lips and licked his jaws when he saw them! After the Leopardess had eaten her evening meal she retired to bed, and the Dog secreted the choicest bones and promised himself a splendid meal next day.

"Next morning as usual the Leopardess went out to hunt,

leaving the Dog alone with the cubs. 'Now,' said the
Dog, smacking his lips, 'I'll have those bones. Dear me,
what a meal I'll have!' and his mouth watered at the
very thought of it. He took the cubs and laid them in the
sun, near the mouth of the cave, and stealing off to
the place in the back of the cave where he had hidden his

treasures, he selected a big shin bone, full of marrow, with
juicy little bits of meat sticking to it. Taking it in his
mouth he carried it to the entrance of the cave, and sitting
down began his meal.

"Ah! how good it tasted! and he smacked his lips again.

"But the floor was a little uneven, and the sand stuck to
the marrow and spoilt its taste, so little by little he shifted

and wriggled himself ahead, until at last he had edged himself to the very mouth of the cave.

"There just ahead of him, a few feet only from the entrance of the cave, he saw a little patch of green sward. It looked so inviting, as the sun fell warmly and lovingly upon it, that he said to himself, 'Ah, that's just the place for me to enjoy my bone,' and, forgetting the Leopardess' warning, he carried the bone out of the cave.

"How velvety and soft the grass felt as the Dog lay down with a sigh of content, and taking the bone between his paws gave it a preliminary lick.

"But what happened to the bone? It would not keep still! The Dog attempted to seize it, but it evaded him and began leaping in every direction as if possessed. Up and down, in and out it leapt, pursued by the Dog, until just as he thought he had caught it, the bone, giving one final bound, struck Tomba, one of the leopard cubs on the head and killed him on the spot.

"'What *shall* I do now?' exclaimed the Dog, horror-stricken, as he gazed ruefully at the dead body of poor little Tomba. If Mistress returns and finds out what I have done she will surely kill me. The best thing I can do is to run away as fast as I can and get out of reach before she returns," and suiting the action to the words, the Dog turned to fly.

"But it was too late, for as he reached the entrance of the cave he saw the Leopardess advancing towards him. The only thing now left for him to do was to hurry back into the cave and put the cubs to bed. He had hardly done so before the Leopardess entered.

"The Dog wagged his tail obsequiously and said 'Good afternoon, Mistress, you are back early to-day, have you not been successful out hunting?'

"'No,' answered the Leopardess shortly. 'Nothing seems to go right to-day. I just missed catching a fat antelope, and almost immediately afterwards I got a thorn in my foot, but I knew there was plenty of giraffe meat left over from yesterday, so I returned home; I shall do no more hunting to-day. I don't know what it is, but I feel as if something had gone wrong. Are Kenyi and Tomba well?' And the Leopardess threw herself discontentedly down on the floor of the cave and called for her cubs.

"'Yes, Mistress,' cried the Dog, 'they are quite well, I will bring them to you one by one.'

"The Dog went to the bed, and taking Kenyi in his arms, laid him at his mother's breasts. When he had sucked his fill the Leopardess called for Tomba. The Dog then carried off Kenyi, and made as if to put him to bed, but brought him back and laid him at his mother's breasts,

me?' shouted the Leopardess, and her suspicions being aroused, she sprang to the bedside and saw lying there the dead body of Tomba.

"With a howl of fury she turned upon the Dog, and just caught sight of him as he shot out of the door of the cave and sped across the plain.

"'Traitor!' shrieked the Leopardess, as she bounded after him, and then the chase began.

"Up hill and down dale they went, the Dog in front and the

hoping she would not notice the deception. The Leopardess, however, turning to caress the cub, noticed at once that it was Kenyi who was again lying beside her.

"'What trick are you playing

Leopardess closely following him, the fire of fury darting from her eyes making her terrible indeed. On and on they went, over rocks and boulders, through streams and bushes, till the Dog's tongue hung out from his mouth and his breath came and went in painful gasps. At last, when he was wellnigh exhausted, and the Leopardess was close upon him, he spied a wart-hog's burrow, and into this he shot for refuge. The Leopardess strove in vain to follow him, for the entrance was too small, and she stood glaring at the Dog, who sat panting just out of her reach.

"'I'll be even with you yet!' roared the Leopardess, lashing her tail furiously at finding herself baffled. Looking round to find some way of getting at the Dog, she saw seated on the bough of a tree close by, a monkey, who was an interested spectator of the scene.

"'Ah! I have him now!' thought the Leopardess, and she called out to the Monkey, 'Monkey, Monkey, come here; I want you to help me, but if you refuse to aid me, or play me false, I will kill you on the spot.' The Monkey, in fear and trembling, promised to help her, and asked her what he should do.

"'I want you,' said the Leopardess, 'to stand here and keep watch over the Dog while I go and collect some sticks to burn him alive in the hole. If he attempts to escape call out, and I will be after him like lightning.'

"'Very well, Mistress,' replied the Monkey, 'you may depend upon me.' And he took up his position as watcher at the mouth of the burrow.

"Away went the Leopardess to gather sticks, and no sooner was her back turned than the Dog called out, 'Monkey, Monkey, you wouldn't be hard on a poor fellow who has done you no harm! I know many of your family, and we have always been friends together. Pray let me out of this hole before the Leopardess returns!'

"'I don't want to harm you," replied the monkey, "I have no grudge against anyone, but if the Leopardess comes back and finds you gone she will surely turn and kill me.'

"'Nay,' said the Dog, 'pretend that I am still in the hole, and when the Leopardess returns, drop the sticks in. She will never know that I am not here. Do but let me out, and I will show you a dell, known only to myself, where grow the choicest nuts!'

"The Monkey was not a bad fellow at heart, in spite of his mischievous ways, and the Dog's promise made him still more well disposed towards him, so he stood aside and the Dog dashed off into the bushes.

"Almost immediately the Leopardess returned, bearing a large bundle of dry twigs.

" ' Is the Dog safe ? ' cried she.

" ' Oh, yes, Mistress, he is safe enough,' answered the Monkey, 'give me the sticks.' And the Monkey, seizing the bundle, dropped the twigs into the hole, and with them he also dropped some hickory nuts he had in his pouch.

" In a short time the burrow was quite full of sticks, and the Leopardess having set fire to them, sat down to witness the burning of Tomba's murderer.

" As the flames burned up the hickory nuts began to crack.

" ' Listen, Mistress ! ' exclaimed the Monkey, 'how his bones are crackling. Oh, but he is having a hot time down there ! '

" ' Ah ! ' roared the Leopardess, ' I swore I would have my revenge.'

" Now all would have gone well," continued Murabo, " if the Dog had behaved with simple common sense. But, Master, he was as curious as a woman and wanted to see how his plan worked. So, instead of making off as fast as he could, he returned to a little hillock close by, and peeped over a stone to see what was going on.

" But just at that very moment the Leopardess happened to look up, and catching sight of him, uttered a roar and was after him again like a streak of light. This time there

seemed no hope for the Dog, for
he was already tired. Away
they went across the plain, and
the Monkey at last lost sight of
them as they swept over a hill.
The Dog held on until he could
almost feel the Leopardess'
breath on his flanks, when suddenly in the distance he caught sight of a
native village, with a number of people sitting
smoking round the fires. Gathering together
all his strength he made for the village, and
slipping through the palisade, took refuge in
one of the huts, where he fell down
exhausted.

"The infuriated Leopardess tried
to follow him, but the villagers,
who loved fair play,
took his part, for he

was the smaller of the two, and seizing their spears, after a fierce fight they slew the Leopardess before his eyes. The Dog was so grateful to the natives for protecting him, that he passed his life amongst them, and died at a good old age, with his children and grandchildren around him.

"Ever since then," continued Murabo, "dogs have preferred to live with the children of men, knowing that they were their best friends. The natives, growing accustomed to having dogs about them, began taming other animals, such as cattle and goats and chickens, and thus it came to pass how animals were first used for domestic purposes."

"Yes, Murabo has told the story well; all that he says is true," exclaimed Abedi, stroking Randy affectionately, "and that is the reason, though we are Mahomedans, we all like dogs."

"Yes," added Raschid, who could not bear to be left out of the conversation, "most Mahomedans do not care greatly for dogs, and consider them unclean animals. I remember when I was a boy in Muscat if we wished to insult anyone we called him "Kelb" (dog), but we in Zanzibar love our dogs, for we remember that it is thanks to a Dog we first had domestic animals."

"Eh, Baba," put in Abedi, "you know my dog Pensil, in Zanzibar, and how I love him. He follows me about all

day, and at night he creeps into bed with me. Ah, poor
Pensil, but he'll be old by the time I get back to Ungujia."
And Abedi heaved a deep sigh as the recollection of his
home in far-off Zanzibar floated across his mind.

The men, too, seemed struck by the same train of
thought, and a silence fell upon the group. So, wishing to
put an end to their broodings, we broke up the meeting,
and returned to the Fort.

CHAPTER V.

OWARDS the end of March a gloom came
over our life at the Fort. Captain Stairs had
left us and had gone down river a month's
journey to Ugarrowa's to bring back the sick
men we had left there to the Fort. Captain Nelson was
prostrated with fever, and our leader, Mr. Stanley, was
suddenly struck down with an illness which wellnigh proved
fatal.

Dr. Parke was very busy in those days, and his entire
time was taken up in attending on Mr. Stanley, Captain
Nelson, and our sick Zanzibaris. How we blessed our
stars that he was with us; how anxiously we looked for
his coming and going, and hung upon his words as if he
were an oracle! The gloomy feeling extended itself to
the men, who went listlessly about their work, and asked
anxiously for news of the B'wana M'Kubwa's (Big Master's)
condition. The one thought in each mind was "what will

become of the Expedition if anything happens to our Leader."

We thought of Major Barttelot and the rear column far away; of our sick men, with Captain Stairs, many days distant; of ourselves at the Fort, with the main body of the men; and of Emin Pasha, waiting anxiously for help. In spite of ourselves, gloomy and depressing thoughts would steal over us, and more and more anxiously we hung on Dr. Parke's words, as we came from our Leader's bedside.

Work, however, and action is the panacea for uncertainty and brooding, and we went to work with a will. There was still much to be done at the Fort, and I kept the men hard at it all day. One party digging a deep trench and raising earthworks, another building an outer stockade and generally improving the defences of the Fort; while a third party continued to clear more land for planting corn and beans.

The only thing to be done was to keep the men at work, just as if our Leader were well, and to speak as little as possible about his illness to the men, and pretend it was nothing serious. The work went on therefore as usual, and at the end of each day's work I went and sat by my Leader's bedside, and told him what had been done and how the work was progressing.

Uledi fully shared our anxiety, but had sense enough not to show it to the men, and he had promised me to do all he could to help me to keep up their spirits.

Sunday came round, and all the morning I was in my Leader's sick room. In the afternoon we met as usual under the tree and I, being the only officer there that day, called upon Uledi for the promised story of Kintu. He was, I could see, taking our Leader's illness very much to heart, and seemed disinclined to speak when the men urged him to begin.

Looking at him, I said, " Uledi, I particularly wish you to tell a story to-day ; remember what you promised me." He understood at once, and answered, " Eh, Walah-Bwana, I will try, but I am no story-teller. If it is work you want, a coxswain for the boat, or somebody to lead the men, I'm ready ; but as to telling a story, Bah, Master, what can I do !" And he shrugged his shoulders and turned the palms of his hands towards us, with a gesture expressive of deprecation.

"Marwee!" cried the man jeeringly, " Who is it we look to to help us when we are in trouble ? who is it cheers us up and makes us laugh when our hearts are down in our stomachs? who is it we call Shaurihamseen (Fifty Plans) because of his cleverness? Why, even our little masters themselves go to you sometimes for counsel when they are

in doubt! You are too modest, Uledi, begin without more
talk, and keep your breath for the story." And the men
began to pelt him with bits of stick.

A gleaming row of white teeth was revealed, as a grin
came over Uledi's ugly, pock-marked face—albeit a face we
all loved—and, warding off the sticks thrown at him, he
began his story without more ado.

"It is an old legend, master, which I learnt many years
ago, when I was little more than a kijana (youth). It was
during my first expedition with the Bwana M'Kubwa, when
he first sailed down the river Congo. Allah! What a
journey that was, and how the Pagans fought us, and
shouted to us that they would have meat that night for
their cannibal feast! It was when we were at Rubaga, and
the Bwana M'Kubwa was the guest of M'Tesa the king.
I will try to relate the story as it was told me by an old
man who was a sweeper in M'Tesa's palace. He called it
Hadithi Ya Kintu.'

(*The Story of Kintu.*)

"In days gone by, many scores of generations ago, before
the world was as it now is, and when crime and bloodshed
were unknown, there lived a man called Kintu, a gentle,
holy, and guileless man, whose heart was as that of a little
child.

"Now Kintu and his wife—whose name I do not remember—were wandering in search of a land in which they
might dwell and till the soil. After many years' wandering
in the wilderness, they came to a country on the shores of
the great lake Nyanza, which is now called Uganda. It
was a beautiful country, Master, with rich fertile valleys,
watered by the clearest streams. The hills were covered
with grass and trees, and the breezes from the Nyanza
blew over them at night, making them fresh and cool.
Allah! It was a veritable Paradise!

"Now Kintu and his wife brought with them to Uganda a
cow, a sheep, a goat, a chicken, a grain of matama, a banana
root, and a sweet potato, and with these they began their
work. They planted the roots in the rich soil, and immediately there grew up vast fields of potatoes and corn and
great green groves of bananas, which yielded large bunches
of luscious fruit. The cow, the sheep, the goat and
chicken were so prolific that soon there sprang up great
flocks and herds of cattle, sheep and goats, and chickens
were as plentiful as the grass of the plain. Kintu's wife,
too, bore him sons and daughters, until Uganda was
peopled by his children and grandchildren, who tilled the
soil and milked the cattle and goats. Some of his children
moved away to the West, taking with them sweet potatoes,
which they planted in the soil. That, Master, is why to

"KINTU AND HIS WIFE BROUGHT WITH THEM TO UGANDA A COW, A SHEEP, A GOAT, AND A CHICKEN."

this day the sweet potato is most eaten in Unyoro. Those who moved north planted the grains of corn, and that is why to this day the Shulis grow matama.

"And Kintu and his wife kept the bananas, which now grow so plentifully in Uganda and Usoga, and his children built themselves fine basket-work huts, and made large villages, round which they planted shady plantain groves, and here they dwelt in peace and plenty.

"Kintu ruled over his people with kindness and wisdom, and as the sun set over the waters of the glorious Nyanza, he looked out from his palace on the hill of Rubaga, over the peaceful land, with a happy and contented heart, and he found that his work was good, for there was no country in the length and breadth of the land so happy and prosperous as Uganda.

"But as the years rolled on, and Kintu grew to be an old, old man, a change came over the land. The people became slothful and wicked; too much prosperity had spoiled them, even as it does us to-day. Is it not true, Master, if we become too rich and have no care or trouble, we become selfish and slothful, thinking only of ourselves and our stomachs? We grow to be lazy, wicked, and quarrelsome, and Shaitan enters our hearts and drives out love and charity.

"And thus it was with the people of Uganda in that far-off

time. They became lustful and envious, and grew bananas only to make wine, which intoxicated and maddened them. The son rose up against his father ; the daughter became wicked and cursed her mother ; each man turned against his neighbour to rob and pillage and kill, until the whole land was drenched with blood ; and the wailing of the helpless rose up to Kintu's throne, and cried out for protection and mercy. In vain did the good old man appeal to the people, and exhort them to return to their former virtuous life ; they only scoffed at and mocked him, and at last answered him even by threats.

"The old man sat in his lonely palace on the hill of Rubaga and talked sadly to his wife of his ruined hopes and the wickedness of their children. They thought of the peaceful and happy days that were past, and of what Uganda had been in the old days, when crime and blood-shed were unknown. Then despair entered Kintu's heart, for he felt that his work had been vain.

"At last he said to his wife, 'This land of Uganda, oh wife, is no more a home for us, there is no longer place or part for us in the life here. Whithersoever I turn I see bloodshed and cruelty, and my ears are tortured by sounds of war and woe, of weeping and lamentation. The young men no longer listen to my words, my counsel falls on un-heeding ears, for their hearts are hardened by wickedness ;

wheresoever I go all men turn from me and draw away with looks of mistrust and hate.

" ' Come, wife, let us be going. Let us rise up and depart

from this wicked land, we will not return until bloodshed and cruelty have ceased.'

"Going out from his palace, he took a last look over the beautiful land—still beautiful—but alas! given up now to cruelty and lust. He stretched out his hands yearningly over his beloved country and lifted up his voice and wept. Then, turning to his wife, he said, ' Come, wife, the day-light is past, let us be going.   We will take with us only our original cow, sheep, goat, chicken, banana and potato roots—perchance we may yet find a land where bloodshed and cruelty are unknown.'

" And so, as the night fell, the Blameless Kintu and his old wife passed away, hand in hand, into the Great Unknown.

  * * * * * *

" When morning was come, the news spread abroad that Kintu and his wife had departed, and sounds of fear and lamentation were heard throughout the land.   The people were sore afraid now that he was gone, and feared lest some evil should befal the country ; the blindness fell from their eyes, and at last they understood all that he had been to them, and bitterly bemoaned their loss.

" For many months they searched for Kintu, but in vain, they found him not.   And the Blameless Kintu, their Priest, Patriarch and King, was no more seen in the fair land of Uganda.

" But soon troubles of war fell on Uganda, and a plague swept over the land.   Strong men were stricken down with a sore disease ; the women as they went to draw water from the well fell by the wayside, and the children sickened and died. Till the voice of the people rose up in a mighty wail, and they cried out in terror and agony, 'Oh! why did we let Kintu go! It is our wickedness which has driven him away and brought a curse upon the land.'

"Then they searched again yet more diligently for their father, but alas! they found him not, for he had vanished from the land.

"And so king succeeded king and sat upon the throne of Uganda; but as the years rolled on the people never forgot their father Kintu, and each successive king searched for him in all the surrounding countries, for there was a belief among the people that Kintu was immortal and would one day return to Uganda.

"Now, after many generations, a king called Ma'anda came to the throne: he was a just king and full of wisdom. In the days of his childhood, as he sat by his mother's knee, he heard from her lips the story of Kintu, and how, through the wickedness of the people, he had departed from the land and been no more seen. As he grew in years he heard it, too, from the old servants about his father's house, and it took strong hold upon his mind. When he grew older he took a seven days' journey down the lake, to the huts of the wise men, who charmed away evil spirits and brought the rain, and they too told him the story. The boy seemed never weary of listening to the legend, and sometimes he would wander off by himself in the forest and ponder deeply over all that he had heard. And so, day by day, a resolve grew up in his heart that when he became king he would rule his country so wisely that bloodshed should cease, and he would search yet more diligently than any other king for the Patriarch Kintu.

" Under his rule Uganda became peaceful and happy once more, and cruelty and murder were at last banished from the land. At each new moon he went long journeys into the forests and mountains of distant Unyoro and Usoga, accompanied only by his faithful Katikiro (prime minister), so that the people, thinking he followed the chase, called him Ma'anda the Hunter. But it was not for the beasts of the forest that he hunted, for the one thought that lay ever at his heart was, ' Oh, if I could but find my father Kintu.'

" Now one day as evening fell and the setting sun lit up the waves of the Nyanza, touching the distant peaks of Usoga with golden red, Ma'anda sat outside his palace on the hill of Rubaga brooding sadly. The scene pleased him not, and in his breast there was no joy for ruling over so fair a land, for his heart was sore within him because he could not find Kintu ; and he stretched out his hands towards the distant mountains and cried in silent prayer, ' Father, have I not obeyed thy commands ? Have I not banished murder and bloodshed from the land? Yet hast thou turned away from me. Kintu, my father—where art thou?'

"And even as he stretched out his hands the faithful

"SPEAK QUICKLY THY MESSAGE."

Katikiro came into his presence, and bowing to the ground before him, said, ' May peace be with thee, my Master, as incessantly as the flowing of waters. A strange peasant has just come from a distant country towards the setting sun, saying he has a message for thee, O King, and it is for thine ears only—may his tidings bring thee peace.'

"Trembling with eagerness, Ma'anda commanded the stranger to be brought before him, and soon the King and the peasant stood alone in the twilight on the hill of Rubaga. Eagerly the King asked, 'What news hast thou brought? Speak quickly thy message, for I am weary of waiting for the tidings my heart tells me thou hast brought at last.'

"The peasant bowed before him and said, 'Thy servant will speak quickly that which he has to tell thee. Many days ago, O King, I was hunting in the forest near my home beyond distant Unyoro, by the banks of the swift M'werango, but that day the antelope kept far from my feet, and wandering on till sunset I came to a mossy dell. There were great trees round it, through the branches of which the sunbeams fell, and from the middle of the soft greensward rose a spring of crystal clear water. The water bubbled up from the middle, and made the pure white sand dance and play at the bottom of the fountain. A clear bright stream ran from it, and laughed and sang in the sunshine as it flowed over the pebbles and was lost in the forest beyond. Ah! King! never have I seen a spot so beautiful.

"'And as I drank eagerly from the spring, a feeling of

drowsiness crept over me, and lying down at the foot of a great tree I fell into a deep sleep, and as I slept I dreamed a dream. An old man with a snow-white beard stood before me, saying, "Rise up and go into the country of Uganda, and tell my words to King Ma'anda. Say that an old man awaits him here who will give him good tidings, which will make his heart leap for joy. He must follow thee to this place, accompanied only by his mother. Tell him not a servant, not even a dog must he bring with him, but only his mother and thee."

"'Thrice did the dream come to me,' continued the peasant, 'and I journeyed day and night to bring thee the message. And this is what thy servant hath to tell thee.'

"'It is Kintu, my father!' cried Ma'anda, and the tears rolled down his cheeks. 'Thou shalt be rich, O peasant, and thy name made honourable in the land.' Then the King, rejoicing, told his mother the story, and the three, taking only a little food with them, stole off secretly by night to the forest.

"But the faithful Katikiro had been watching them, and fearing lest harm should befall his beloved master, he seized his spear and followed them from afar unseen. Day and night they journeyed on for many days; at every fresh opening in the forest Ma'anda turned to see that no one was following, but the Katikiro watched carefully, and

G

always hid himself behind a tree and kept from his master's sight.

" At last, led by the peasant, they came to the mossy dell, and there before them, seated upon the grass, they saw a circle of old men clad in white robes. In front of them was one with a snow-white beard, more venerable than the rest, who rose as Ma'anda approached.

" ' Who art thou ? ' he asked in a clear, sweet voice, ' and from whence hast thou come ? '

" ' I am Ma'anda, King of Uganda,' answered the King.

" ' And who is this woman with thee ? '

" ' She is my mother, whom thou hast commanded me to bring.'

" ' And hast thou brought no one with thee but thy mother and this peasant ? ' demanded the old man.

" ' No one but these two,' answered Ma'anda.

" ' It is well,' said the sage, ' for the words I have to say are for thine ears only. My son, I am thy father Kintu. Bloodshed and violence drove me from my beloved country, and I vowed I would not return until they had ceased, and a king should reign *upon whose hands there was no stain of blood.* I have watched thee, my son, with love in my heart, for I have seen how bravely thou hast struggled against the temptations that beset thee, and how nobly thou hast striven to banish murder from the land. I have

"SEATED ON THE GRASS, THEY SAW A CIRCLE OF OLD MEN CLAD IN WHITE ROBES."

seen how thou hast searched for me, a hundredfold more than any other king, and how thou hast kept all my commandments, and my heart went out to thee to see how nobly thou hast borne the test. And now, my son, the time has come when '—— But here the old man stopped suddenly, saying, 'Thou hast deceived me—who is this man behind thee?'

"Ma'anda turned and saw the Katikiro, who had crept up to hear what the old man was saying. With a cry of rage he bounded towards him, and seizing the spear from his hand he drove it into the heart of his faithful servant. The Katikiro, with a groan, immediately fell, *and his blood flowed out over the hands of Ma'anda.*

"'Ah! Woe is me,' cried Kintu ; '*there is blood even upon thy hands,*' and even as Ma'anda turned, Kintu and the elders, with a cry of horror, vanished from his sight while their voices rang out through the forest, 'Woe! Woe! Woe! to the bloody land of Uganda!'

"Ma'anda and his mother rent their clothes in despair, and cried wildly for Kintu to return, but the wind only answered through the tree-tops, 'Woe! Woe! Woe!'

"And so," continued Uledi, "Ma'anda and his mother returned sadly to their home, and from that day to this Kintu has never more been seen, nor will he appear again until bloodshed has ceased in Uganda."

*   *   *   *   *   *

The men were all greatly struck with the story, and for awhile we were silent.   Uledi had told the tale most vividly, using the quaint figures of speech with which the Zanzibaris usually garnish their narrations.   He seemed to feel it all deeply, and as he repeated the tale in a low voice his ugly

face had grown softened and troubled, till he seemed to be almost good-looking.

Binza was the first to break the silence.   "Ah! the people of Uganda did not know how happy they were in having such a king to rule over them until he had gone. It is always so : there are times when our old people annoy us and seem to thwart our wishes, and then in our anger we rebel against them, and think that we ourselves know much better than they; there are times even when we almost wish that they were gone. And yet, when they *are* gone, remorse knocks at our hearts till, like the people of Uganda, we cry out in our sorrow, " Ah! why did we let our anger burn hot against them ; why did we not love and value the old people whom Allah in his goodness had given us?"

" Ay!" said the men, " it is always so : we never knew how much we all cared for Khamis-kururu until he was gone, and we used sometimes to think him a tiresome, talkative, lazy old man. But when death took him we remembered his kindly ways and missed his cheerful voice about the camp. Then we recollected the good advice he had often given us, and the thought of the many kind things he had done rose up in our hearts and choked us as we dug his grave on the banks of the Ihuru river, and left him lying there, far from his home, with only Pagans around him. Eh, Wallah Bwana, surely we should value our old people while they are with us, and do our best to make their lives peaceful and happy, lest Allah in his anger should take them from us and leave our hearts sorrowing and full of remorse."

" You speak with akilli " (sense), exclaimed Murabo, " we never value our old men as we ought when we see that they can no longer run and hunt and have no strength. But their heads are generally wiser than ours and their advice worth listening to. I will tell you all a story about an old man and five young men who thought they were wiser than he ; but that story will do for another day when we and the Masters meet here again together, and when Inshallah (by the grace of God) the Bwana M'Kubwa is recovered. We get so used to seeing our old people with us that we do not understand how things would be without them."

" Ay, verily," cried all the men, "what should we do without M'seh (old man) Raschid. He is no longer as quick and strong as he used to be, but he is our father and mother, and the old man's advice is always good. Truly we should be uneasy if we did not see his face among us. How do you treat your old people, Master, in Ulaiah ? " (Europe).

And I answered I was sorry to say that we did not always value them and treat them as we should, and that white men as well as black had much to learn from the story of Kintu.

CHAPTER VI.

THE STORY OF DAOUD THE FISHERMAN.

ON SUNDAY, March 11th, 1888, I see in my journal the following entry:

"This morning at 3.30 we were all turned out of our beds by an invasion of red ants, and most of us were frightfully bitten. We rushed out of our huts stamping and beating ourselves and tearing off our night clothes in our wild endeavours to get rid of the ants, which had swarmed all over our legs and were biting us viciously. The poor goats, which were tied to the granary, were nearly driven mad, so we had to let them loose, and could hear them running about in the darkness bleating piteously."

Now one of the pests which troubled us at the Fort were these red ants. None of the plagues of Egypt in the days of Moses and Pharoah could have been worse than the plague of these biting, ferocious ants. They made their nests in holes deep down under ground, but at certain times they would issue forth in millions from their nests and travel round ; sometimes they would go a distance of half a mile in search of food.

They preferred travelling along the pathways, but nothing stopped their progress. One would see sometimes what, at a little distance, looked like a long reddish coloured rope, about two inches broad, stretched along the ground, but when you approached this seeming rope you found it to be a moving line, formed of millions and millions of red ants. On examining them, you found there were two kinds, the workers and the warriors. They always travelled together, the workers in the middle, protected by the warriors, who marched on either side of them. The workers were comparatively small, but the warrior ants were quite half an inch long, and had enormous mandibles or nippers, with which they seized upon any living thing which came across their line of march. Sometimes when we were marching, the men would unwarily step amongst them, and the whole caravan would be routed by the furious attack these red ants immediately made upon them ; the men would throw down their loads and dash into the bushes, madly trying to beat them off. It was useless attempting to brush them away, for they held on far too tightly, and even if you pulled their bodies in two, their heads would still hang on and continue to bite. And so you may imagine all living things fled before them and gave them a wide berth. If they are passing near a hut, and smell anything good to eat, they immediately swarm into it and never leave off until they have eaten up everything. If they cannot find the door they come in through the roof or search for a hole or chink in the wall, through which they pour like a stream of reddish brown water. The only way in which to stop them is by emptying burning ashes about the floor, but they generally find another way round. I myself have sometimes sat up half the night surrounded by a little circle of burning ashes, waiting till the red ants, which swarmed all over the camp, had gone.

One good thing they do is to clear out all the cockroaches, rats, and mice they find in the hut, into which they go ; they make a clean sweep of everything, so that after one of their visits the hut is for a while entirely free from vermin.

There was a bird in the forest which the Zanzibaris used to call the ant-bird, because they said it used to call out to the ants where food was to be found. It had a peculiar note, which the men interpreted thus :

> " N' jo ! N' jo ! N' jo !
> Watu ! hapa ! watu !
> Chakula siafu n' jo ! "

which in English means :

"Come, ants, come !
Here are some people !
Come and eat the food !"

And then the men told us the bird hopped about the trees
and waited till the ants had eaten their fill, and then, as pay-
ment for telling them where the food was, would suddenly
pounce down and make its own meal on a hundred or two
of the ants themselves.

Many of the birds and animals in the forest round the
Fort used to make very curious sounds, which at a short
distance sounded almost human.

There were big Chimpanzee monkeys which looked like
fat old men and women ; they were as big as the dwarfs
themselves.   Sometimes we heard the little ones crying up
in the trees just like children ; we could hear the old ones
scolding them, just as if they were telling them they were
wicked, undutiful children.   And then the little monkeys
cried again still more, and seemed to realize how bad they
were.   We were seldom able to see them, for the branches
were interlaced so thickly together that it was like another
world, away up far above our heads, among those great
high tree tops.   Still, if we kept quiet, we could often hear
them laughing and playing and quarrelling together, just
like so many human beings.

I remember one day we were rowing up the Aruwimi

river in our boat the "Advance," and we passed by a place
where a number of huge apes were leaping from tree to tree

in a long procession. When they saw us they evidently
wondered who we could be, for they came and sat on a
bough overhanging the water, and watched us gravely.

They looked so funny, sitting in a row with their arms round each other's necks, and their tails hanging straight down. Then two great big red monkeys, the patriarchs of the family, came down lower and chattered at us ; they seemed to be making rude, personal remarks about our appearance, for all the rest of the family immediately joined them, shaking the boughs on which they were sitting and making faces at us ; it seemed just as if they were jeering at and mocking us. We looked down at our tattered clothes and felt absolutely ashamed, and for the first time realized what ragged, dirty objects we must be. We absolutely blushed, for those monkeys put us quite out of conceit with ourselves and made us feel our inferiority. We all seemed struck dumb with shame, and pulled on as fast as we could to get out of reach of their rude and ill-bred remarks !

I recollect on this particular Sunday, seven of our men, whom we had left because they were sick, some months before, in a Manyema slave-raiders' camp, arrived at the Fort. Poor fellows ! they were perfect skeletons, and they told us terrible stories of the cruelty they had experienced in the slavers' camp. Our Zanzibaris were delighted to see them again, and nearly killed them with kindness. They stuffed them with ripe bananas and goat's meat, and all crowded round them to watch how much they enjoyed having food again. They would not allow them to stop eating, until at last, after being nearly dead from starvation, they were in danger of being killed by too much food. Our Leader, Mr. Stanley, was still very ill, and could not yet be moved, but his illness had taken a change for the better, and we were all in good spirits with the news the doctor had given us of his improved condition.

That afternoon we met as usual under the tree, and some of the men, who had that day come in from the slavers' camp, came and sat with us, and told us such stories about the Manyema that the men were all furious and indignant. We talked of what we ourselves had suffered from them ; of the time when we, a mere handful of tattered and half starved strangers, had arrived at their village of Ipoto, and been robbed by them.

No words of abuse were strong enough for our Zanzibaris to describe in fitting terms what they thought of them, and when all other words had failed, they ended up, as they usually did, by exclaiming, with a shrug of their shoulders " Bah ! Masters, what else could we expect from Pagans ! "

" But," we exclaimed, " the Manyema profess to be Mahomedans ! "

" Nay, Masters," exclaimed Kheri, one of our chiefs, " you must not think the Manyema are true sons of Islam, and really know anything about the Prophet ; they are at heart nothing but Pagans, just as some of the white men are on the West Coast, who profess to be followers of the Nazarene. The Prophet teaches us to be kind to all strangers who come to us in trouble, and tells us it is one of the things which is most pleasing to Allah. True sons of Islam should always be kind to strangers in distress."

"Eh Wallah, Abdullah," exclaimed Uledi, "can you not remember the story of Daoud, which our mothers used to tell us years ago. Tell it to the Masters now, and they will see what we, the true sons of Islam, are taught about hospitality even when we are children."

"Yes, Abdullah," we all cried, "tell it to us, for it is your turn to-day for a story."

"Bah, Masters," interrupted Laki, who was one of the wits of the camp, "I don't know what sort of hand Abdullah is at telling a story, but I know he is a *fundi* at the cooking pots. He eats more food on Jumah Tato (Sunday) than would last me for the whole week. On Sundays he is usually '*sheba sana*' (quite full), and is only fit to sleep."

This sally of Laki's called forth a laugh from us all, for Abdullah's love for the flesh-pots was proverbial. However, unlike most greedy people, he was very good-natured, so nothing abashed, he laughed good humouredly and exclaimed, "Hold your tongue then, Laki, and be silent while I tell the Masters the story of Daoud the Fisherman, and how, through his kindness and hospitality to a stranger in trouble, he gained his King's gratitude and became ruler over all his household.

"Long, long ago, before Said Said came over from Arabia and conquered the land, making Zanzibar an Arab country, the kingdom of Ungujia consisted of several different countries and islands, and each had its own king and court.

"Far away to the south of Zanzibar lay an island, called Combro, the first ruler of which was a king named Saphoom.

"He was a wise king, and was much beloved by his subjects, over whom he ruled in a firm and beneficent manner. It was a beautiful and rich island, with great mango and cocoa-nut groves growing down to the sea shore, just as there are, Masters, in Zanzibar. You have seen them there and know how beautiful they are, and how the children play under the thick shade of the mangoes, which grow up in dark green billowy masses high up like mountains, with the orange trees among them, laden with bright golden fruit and the cocoa-nut trees leaning lovingly over till their long fan-like leaves almost kiss the water." Here Abdullah heaved a sigh as he drew this picture of far-off Ungujia and thought of his bright, peaceful home among the cocoa-nut and mango groves. How far off it seemed to us all, that day!

"Well, Masters, just such an island as Zanzibar was the island of Combro, and there the King dwelt in his palace by the sea shore with his two wives, Tijara and Hanima. From the windows of the palace he caught glimpses through the palm trees of the bright blue ocean rolling in in great white breakers upon the golden strand. Everything was bathed in sunshine. The cool breeze blew in through the open windows of the King's palace, bringing with it the scent of flowers, the distant sound of the sea, and the gay laughter of the children as they played in the surf on the beach below.

"And as evening was falling, the King would stand with his two wives and watch his boats as they sailed gaily home in the setting sun, laden with rich spices and stuffs which they brought from the merchants of Ungujia and the mainland.

"Allah! Masters, how beautiful it all was, and what a happy, peaceful life Saphoom led in his island out on the great blue ocean.

"Now the King loved both his wives; but he loved Tijara best, for she was so beautiful, and gentle, and kind, and was beloved by all who approached her, by reason of her kindly gracious ways. But Hanima saw this, and was

SAPHOOM AND HIS WIVES.

consumed with jealousy, for she perceived that the King cared more for a glance from Tijara than for all her caresses. Then Shaitan entered her heart, and day by day she sat in her chamber and brooded how she could ruin Tijara and win all the King's love for herself.

"So one night she secretly stole from the palace and made her way through the darkness to the hut of an old medicine man who lived far away by a lonely swamp in the middle of a great forest. She carefully concealed her face so that the old man might not recognize her, and asked him to give her a strong potion which would plunge the person who drank it into a deep sleep.

"Having obtained the medicine, she hurried back to the palace without anyone knowing where she had been. She crept silently into the chamber where Tijara lay peacefully sleeping. Allah! how beautiful she looked as she lay stretched upon the couch, with her long silken lashes fringing her cheeks, and her beautiful bosom rising and falling as she slept peacefully on, dreaming of Saphoom and of her sweet happy life. But the sight of her beauty only hardened the heart of Hanima, and as she gazed on Tijara's loveliness she became almost mad with jealousy and hate. Leaning over the prostrate form of her rival she gently poured a few drops of the poison between the lips of Tijara, who immediately fell into a stupor.

H

"'Now,' muttered Hanima, 'I will ruin her beauty, so that she shall no longer find favour in the eyes of the King,' and seizing a glittering knife she cut out the eyes of Tijara.

"After a few hours the effect of the poison wore off and Tijara awoke, and putting her hands to her eyes she found she was blind.   As she sprang from her couch she heard the taunting voice of Hanima near her, saying, 'Now, oh hateful Tijara, I have destroyed thine eyes, thou art no longer beautiful, the King will turn from thee with loathing, and will transfer all his love to me.'

"'Ah!' moaned the wretched woman, 'what have I done to thee that thou hast destroyed my life and made the world darkness to me for ever?'

"'Done!' hissed Hanima, 'hast thou not stolen from me the love of my lord, and turned his heart against me, and now I am revenged upon thee.'

"Stung by the taunts of her rival, and maddened with despair for the loss of her beauty, Tijara fled from the palace, followed by the mocking laugh of Hanima.   On and on through the dark night she fled, until she reached the sea-shore, and then with a long, despairing cry she threw herself into the sea and the waters closed over her.

*   *   *   *   *   *

"Now when morning was come, sounds of weeping and

wailing reached the King's ears, and hurrying past the panic-stricken slaves, he came to Tijara's chamber. There surrounded by weeping women, he saw the empty, and blood-stained couch, and he understood that Tijara, the light of his life was dead.

"Then the King rent his clothes, and throwing himself upon the couch, kissed the pillows which had been so recently pressed by the head of his beloved Tijara.

"Then there was a hurrying to and fro of the King's warriors, who searched through the length and breadth of the land for the destroyer of the Queen, but no traces of the murderer were found.

"For many moons the King covered his head and lay upon the ground and refused to be comforted. But the cunning Hanima moved softly round Saphoom, and wept with him; and when the days of mourning were over, the King rose and washed and anointed himself, and took her again to his bosom, and Hanima was content. And so the years rolled on, and Tijara and her sad fate seemed almost to be forgotten by the people. But Saphoom never forgot her, and when at night Hanima lay sleeping beside her lord, he secretly mourned for the loss of his gentle companion, and ceased not to cry in silent prayer, ' Tijara, Tijara, Allah-hu Akabara.'

*　　　*　　　*　　　*　　　*　　　*

"Now hard by the city dwelt a fisherman called Daoud. He lived in a poor hut with his seven daughters in a little

cocoa-nut grove by the sea-shore.　He was very poor, and toiled all day to support himself and his children.　Early in the morning he would be out in his tiny boat setting his nets, and at mid-day it was his custom to carry his fish into the city and sell them for a small piece of money, which he exchanged for rice and 'bizarre' (curry stuffs). But times were hard, for fish were scarce, and for many days he had hardly caught anything, and Daoud began to despair by reason of his ill-luck.

" Now early one morning as he cast his net he felt it was heavy, and his heart leaped with joy, for he thought his ill-luck had turned and at last he had caught a great draught of fishes. What was his surprise on drawing the net to land to find in its meshes a blind but beautiful woman. Then a great fear fell on Daoud when the woman, as if awakening from a long sleep, rose up, and in a sweet voice asked, 'Who art thou, and what is this land upon which I have awakened?'

"'And he answered, 'I am Daoud the fisherman, and this, oh Lady, is the island of Combro.'

"'And who is the ruler of this land?' asked the Stranger.

"'The good King Saphoom is the ruler of the land, and hard by is the palace where he lives with the Queen Hanima.'

"'The Stranger heaved a deep sigh and said : ' Has the King then none other wife than Hanima?'

" ' None other, Lady, than Hanima,' replied Daoud, ' but
I have heard that years ago, when I lived in the island of
Pemba, the king had yet another wife, called Tijara, who
was more beautiful than the day. But one night she
disappeared, and though they searched throughout the
land for her, she was never found. The people say
the King has never been the same since then, for Tijara
was the light of his eyes.'

" Then the Stranger wept bitterly, and clasping her
hands over her sightless eyes, she talked to herself in a
low voice, so low that Daoud could not hear her words ;
but though he was only a rough fisherman his heart was
large, and he tried to comfort her.

" At length the Stranger drying her tears, said, ' Daoud,
mine heart tells me that thine is kind: wilt thou have pity
on a blind woman, and help a stranger who is poor and in
deep distress. Take me to thine house, and may God
reward thee for thy charity.'

" ' Nay, Lady,' said Daoud, ' though my hut is humble
and we are poor, I will turn no stranger in distress from my
door ; who but the poor should help the poor, and such
food and shelter as I have, I offer you in the name of the
Gods,' and taking her by the hand he led her to his hut.

" ' Now when the daughters saw their father bringing the
Stranger home they were wroth, and cried : ' Who is this

Stranger that thou hast brought; hast thou not enough mouths to feed, without taking in a stranger, and that a blind woman?'

And Daoud's daughters began to reproach their father, until the old man knew not what to do.

"But the youngest daughter, the gentle Dahara, with tears of pity in her sweet eyes, exclaimed: 'Nay, father, turn not the Stranger away, there is the little hut close by in the cocoa-nut grove which thou madest last summer for the fishing-nets, let her stay there, and I myself will tend her; it may be that her coming will bring us good luck.'

"Then Dahara led the Stranger to the little hut, and making her a soft bed of sweet-scented grass, told her to lie down and rest. And when the sun became low in the heavens, Dahara taking a portion of her own frugal meal, brought it to the Stranger and bade her eat. · Then saying kind words to her, she called upon the Gods to watch over the helpless woman, and bade her good night.

"Now when the sun rose, and Dahara went to the hut, the Stranger said she wished to bathe, and Dahara brought her a bath and clear cool water from the well in an earthern jar. And as she washed the water fell from her in a flood of gold and silver. It filled the bath and flowed out over the floor, until the poor hut glittered in the morning sun like a king's palace.

" Running to the sea-shore, Dahara told her father what had befallen, and going to the hut they gathered up the gold and silver and hid it in a hole under the hearth.

" For three successive mornings the Stranger washed and

the gold fell from her in streams, until Daoud had stores of gold and silver as large as any noble in the land.

" Now on the fourth day Dahara dreamed a dream. As she slept she heard a voice saying, ' Rise up, my daughter, and go into the city, taking with thee a piece of the gold which has fallen from the Stranger thou hast befriended.

Go into the market-place, and there thou shalt see an old man with a green turban seated upon the ground with his tray of merchandise before him. Give him the piece of gold, and tell him thou comest in the name of the Gods. He will give thee a red fish and a 'piece of 'Oudi' wood. Take them to the hut of the Stranger, and placing the eyes of the fish in her eyes, thou shalt light the 'Oudi' wood and waft the smoke upon them. Do this, and the Gods will reward thee.'

"As soon as Dahara awoke she told her father the dream, and, taking a piece of gold with her, she wended her way towards the city. And there, on entering the market-place she saw an old man with a green turban seated upon the ground, just as the voice in her dream had described him. The old man on seeing her called out that he had bracelets and wares for pretty maidens, and held out towards her yellow amber necklets and glittering beads of gold and silver.

"But Dahara put them aside, and offering the piece of gold said, ' Nay, Baba, I want none of these, for I come in the name of the Gods.'

"'And may they reward thee, gentle maiden, for thy kindly heart,' answered the old man, as he drew out from under his tray a red fish and a piece of 'Oudi' wood, and gave them to Dahara.

"'Assanti Baba, lubda takuyia Kheri,' (thank you, father, it may be good luck will come), she murmured, as she hid them in her kanso, and turned towards her home.

"That night she and her father came quietly into the Stranger's hut, and as she slept they put the red-fish' eyes into hers and wafted the smoke of the 'Oudi' wood around her. Then, with a humble prayer to the Gods to bless their efforts, the gentle girl and her good old father crept silently away.

"With dawn of day Dahara stood by the couch of the Stranger and watched in fear and trembling to see what would befall. And as she watched, the sleeper's lips moved, she stirred uneasily, and raising her hands to her eyes she woke, no longer blind, but restored to all her former glorious beauty. And at the sight of her dazzling beauty Dahara fell on her knees and bowed herself to the ground before her.

"But the Stranger raised her up and kissing her kindly, said :

"'My heart went out towards thee, Dahara, when I, a blind outcast, first heard thy sweet voice pleading with thy father and sisters for the Stranger. Thou knewest not whom thou wast rescuing from despair, but knew only that I was poor and in trouble, and that was enough for thy gentle heart. Surely thy reward shall be great and thy life made rich and happy. Go, fetch thy good old father, that I may look upon his face and thank him for his kindness and hospitality to the Stranger.'

"And when Dahara brought her father to the hut, the Stranger spoke kindly, gracious words to him, and the two bowed low before her, for she was of Queenly Presence.

* * * * * *

"Now hard by Daoud's little plot of land lay a cocoa-nut grove belonging to Najumbi, the King's steward. That morning as Najumbi walked in the grove, he climbed a cocoa-nut tree to gather fruit, and looking over the wall he saw the Stranger washing, and as the sun fell on her he was astonished at her loveliness. Quickly descending from the tree he made his way to the royal palace, and prostrating himself before the King said : 'Master, without offence, I beg to kiss thine hands, and to tell thee what thy servant has seen. As I walked this morning, Oh King, in my cocoa-nut grove by the sea-shore, I became thirsty and climbed a tree to gather some fruit. And there I saw in the garden of Daoud the fisherman a woman more beautiful than the day washing herself before a little hut in the morning sun. And as I gazed some memory of past years rose before me, for the woman seemed to me to be like the lost Queen Tijara—peace be to her memory, only this woman was ten times more beautiful. Then I hastened to come down from the tree and come before thee, oh! King, to tell thee what thy servant has seen.'

"Then the King trembled, for as he looked back through the memory of past days, all his tenderness and love for Tijara welled up in his heart, till he was consumed by love and longing to see the strange woman who was like her. So as the evening fell, the King, disguised as a merchant, made his way to Daoud's hut, accompanied by the steward.

"Entering the house he called for Daoud and told him he had heard that he had a beautiful daughter and commanded him to bring her before him. Daoud, who recognized the King through his disguise, was sore afraid and stricken with fear, for he thought of the Stranger and of the gold, and feared lest it might be found hidden under the hearth and he and his children branded as robbers.

One by one he tremblingly brought his daughters before the King, who impatiently waved each away. At last Dahara came in, and Daoud told the King that she was the youngest, and these daughters, seven in number, were all that he had. The King looked at the gentle Dahara and said, 'Verily, this maiden, thy youngest daughter, is fair to see, but it is not she I seek, thou hast yet another whom thou hast hidden from me. Bring her at once before me or my vengeance shall fall upon thine head.'

"THE STRANGER GLIDED SOFTLY INTO THE ROOM."

"Daoud in terror threw himself at the King's feet, and protested that he had no other daughter, and Dahara sank on her knees before him and begged him to be merciful to her father.

"But the King was wroth, and ordered the Steward to bind him hand and foot and cast him into prison.

"But even as the Steward moved forward to do the King's bidding, the Stranger glided softly into the room.

"Allah! how beautiful she looked, with the flickering lamp light falling upon her, as she stood there before the King, with her hands crossed upon her breast and her sweet eyes cast down. It seemed as if some beautiful spirit had come down from above to that poor fishing-hut upon the sea-shore.

"Then a loud cry of gladness rang out upon the still evening, as the King crying: 'Tijara! Tijara!' Allah-hu-Akabara clasped her in his arms.

"Thus, after long years of separation and mourning, King Saphoom and the long lost Tijara met once more.

*   *   *   *   *   *

"Soon it became known to the people in the city that the dead was living, the lost was found, and that Tijara, their Queen was restored to them.

"Hanima, as she sat in the Palace waiting for Saphoom to return and wondering what kept her lord so long from her side, heard the criers in the streets shouting news abroad, which was answered from all sides by loud acclamations from the people.

"Some instinct of fear made her heart sink, for she fancied she caught the name of Tijara, and creeping from the palace on to the city wall she listened with bated breath.

"And as she listened and strained her ears to catch their words, the crowd came nearer and nearer until at last she heard above the shouts of the people the words of the criers, ' Hadithi ! Hadithi ! Hear oh people the welcome news and rejoice ! This night our Beloved Queen, the beautiful Tijara has been restored to us. Through the wickedness of the cruel Hanima she was driven from us and was lost, but this night, through the goodness of the Gods she has been found by the King in the hut of the fisherman Daoud.'

"Loud cries of joy greeted the words of the criers, and the people, like a mighty flood, streamed out of the city gate to welcome the King and Tijara.

"Then a great fear and trembling took hold upon Hanima, and covering her head she fled through the darkness and cowered, terror-stricken, among the rocks by the sea-shore.

"And soon she heard in the distance a sound of horns

and drums, and the joyful shouts of the people, as they
moved along the sea-shore from Daoud's hut to the King's
palace. And as the procession approached, she saw by the
light of a thousand torches, surrounded by the dancing,

shouting crowd, the King reclining on his litter, and in his
arms was Tijara, more beautiful than ever.

"'I have lived long enough!' hissed Hanima, as with a
cry of fury and hate she leaped from the rocks into the sea;
and the next morning her dead body was washed up upon

the shore at the place where Daoud had drawn the blind Stranger to shore in his net.

"And so it came to pass," continued Abdullah, "that the King in his gratitude made the poor fisherman Daoud ruler over all his house, and Dahara became the chief woman in the Queen's chamber.

"And as time went on, Hanamouri, the King's young brother, took the gentle Dahara for his wife, and she, too, lived in a palace by the sea, and had servants and slaves to do her bidding, and jewels and fine raiment to wear.

"There they dwelt in Combro in happiness and peace. Tijara bore the king sons and daughters, and we, Master, the people of N'gazijah, are the descendants of the good King Saphoom and the beautiful Tijara. This, Masters," concluded Abdullah, "is the story of Daoud the fisherman as it is related to us in Zanzibar by our mothers when we are children. And they tell us that we should remember, like Daoud, to be kind to strangers, lest we turn some one in distress from our doors whom Allah has sent to befriend."

*   *   *   *   *   *

"That is a very pretty story, Abdullah," we all exclaimed, "And we are glad to know that your mothers teach you such things as gratitude and hospitality, for truly they are pleasing to Allah. Know you not what the Hadji Abdullah

(Sir Richard Burton) has said about the Negroes having no gratitude ? "

"Nay, Masters," interrupted Raschid, our head chief, "the white man is not always just to the black, and does not sometimes understand him. We have heard what the Hadji Abdullah has said of us, and we know that many white men in Ulaiya (Europe) are of his mind, too. Yet, Masters, what kind of man is the Hadji Abdullah ? Did he not, after a battle, gather together the heads of his enemies in a sack and send them to Ulaiya, so that all the people gave him the name of 'M'zungu M'baiya ?' (the wicked white man). What care we for his words, even though he says that the black man has not love for his women folk ; neither has he gratitude to those who befriend him, nor affection for his kindred. I know, Master, you and the little Masters would never say such things of us, for we have been through troubles and have faced death together ; it has made us to be of one mind and heart, and the remembrance of many things we have passed through together in the forest will always be in our hearts. Do you not remember, Masters, when Osmani died in the forest in the days of our wanderings, when we fought against hunger and sickness ? Have you forgotten how, when we left him lying there by the path, his last words were of his mother ? Nay, if you have forgotten them I

I

will repeat them, for they will remain ever here in my heart. 'Give my greetings to my mother, and say In-shallah, we shall meet in the land of God.' Those were Osmani's words. Do not believe them, Masters, when they say that the Negro knows not love, and has neither gratitude nor affection ; for we love our mothers, even as the white man does. `Have we not the saying which was brought by our grandfathers from the East, ' Allah cannot be everywhere, therefore he has made mothers ? ' When we are children is it not to our mothers that we always turn ? Is it not she whom we think wiser than all the world, for she tends us lovingly when we are sick and when we are tired with play we love to return to her, to sit by her knee and hear her tell us stories of far away countries and times.

"Then, too, is it not our mother who first tells us of Allah and his goodness, and teaches us to pray to him for all that we need. And, Masters, when our life is ended, and we have reached the boundary of that long and rugged way, where the gates of Paradise stand, and we see—if Allah wills it—those gates roll open before us, whose hand is it but our mother's which has helped us to open them, for she has first given us the key ? And who knows, perhaps, she will be the first to welcome us on the other side when we have passed through the gateway of life and death ?

"We know there are many bad and ungrateful men among us, whose hearts are no bigger than a pebble, who regard none else but themselves, and remember not in their hearts the kindness of others. But what people are there in all the world—whether black or white—who have not bad men among them?

"In-shallah, Masters, if we reach Zanzibar our mothers and sisters, our wives and children and brothers will come down with light in their eyes and love in their hearts to greet us, then you will see if the Negro has not love and affection for his kindred.

"So, B'wana, if when you return to Ulaiya you hear people say that the black man is bad, think of the days of our wanderings together, remember those days of starvation, disaster and sickness ; forget not how the black man held to you, and then tell them by the recollection of all these things, that, though the Negro is rough, ignorant and often wicked, he, too, has a heart and can remember."

"Eh, wallah B'wana," murmured the men, "verily Raschid our father has the gift of speech, he has spoken nothing but the truth, and has told you all that is in our hearts."

CHAPTER VII.

THE STORY OF KILINDI.

HE Fort and its surroundings were now almost completed. Our four big watch towers were finished and roofed in, they looked in the distance like little Swiss Châlets. A big ditch and earthworks had been dug round the Fort and broad pathways and roads had been cut in the banana plantations up to the edge of the forest. Our cornfields too which were our greatest pride, and which promised an abundant crop, had been completely fenced in by high wattled hurdles.

We had now about eleven acres of ground under cultivation ; our beans had been ready some time, and we were just beginning to eat green corn from the field which had only been planted six weeks before. This will give some idea of the rapidity with which things grew in our tropical climate. We had a patch of tobacco growing well, and all our men had their little gardens at the back of their huts in which they grew pot herbs and wild spinach.

In fact, things were now so complete that we felt we might at last think of moving on and trying a second time to reach Emin Pasha. Our leader, Mr. Stanley, had now almost recovered his strength and was able to walk about the Fort and direct the work, as he had been accustomed to before his illness.

We had been working every day except Sundays, for two months, from six in the morning till five at night, and we all felt very proud of our work, for in the middle of that great dark forest, shut away from all the world and surrounded by hostile savages, we had made ourselves a safe and comfortable home. This Sunday morning had however been a sad one to us. Some days before a party of thirty men had been sent out under one of our chiefs, Munia Pembe, to try and find a ford by which we could cross the river Ihuru. That morning they had returned greatly dispirited, carrying in a hammock Munia Pembe, who had been wounded by the savages. They brought the news also that two of our best men, Salimani and Kamweia, had been killed by poisoned arrows.

The men told us that they had all reached the river two days after they started from the Fort and had encamped in a small village, which they found deserted, on the river bank. But that night, when they were sleeping, great numbers of savages had come over in large canoes from the other side of the river, and had attacked them, while another band had crept up in the forest unawares and had fallen upon them from behind.

Salimani and Kamweia had been killed at the first rush, while several others had been wounded, and it had taken them three days to fight their way back to the Fort, for the savages had followed them nearly all the way.

We were all very sad at the news, for so many of our men had already been killed by the natives, and we were now reduced to a small band of men, 180 in all, so small a band that every single friendly face was greatly missed among us. The sick men were tended by Dr. Parke, and Munia Pembe's wound was carefully dressed with medicine which took away the poisonous effect of the arrrow with which he had been struck. Numbers of our men too had been waylaid and killed by the savages who prowled about the forest near by, and now the death of these two had made us feel more than ever how wise we had been to make our Fort safe and strong.

We were talking rather sadly together when we took our pipes that afternoon, and repaired as usual to the shade of our tree. The men were speaking sorrowfully among themselves about Salimani's wife, and Kamweia's mother, whom they knew in Zanzibar, and were saying how sad they would be when we reached Zanzibar and found that they were dead.

Alas! there were many sad hearts on that day when we reached Zanzibar nearly two years later, and the news was told of the death of so many of our faithful men.

Seeing how depressed the men were one of us told them a story, I think it was the story of the Patriarch Abraham with his flocks and herds. After the usual comments had been made upon it by the men, we called upon Khamis Parri, one of our chiefs, for a story. He had travelled about the world a good deal, and spoke several languages, English among them, for he had once been an interpreter on board an English man-o'-war. He at once complied with our request, saying, "M'seh Raschid last Sunday spoke about the goodness and kindness of mothers; I will now tell you a story, Masters, about a step-mother who was wicked and cruel.

" Long years ago, Masters, in the days of the good King Saphoom of Combro, there lay on the sea coast, to the north of Ungujia, a beautiful country called Kilindi. King Munia Pembe ruled over the country, and built his city on that fair tract of land which stands out into the sea in the shape of a man's hand. You may see its form to this day, but now behind it runs the clear, deep harbour, which in the first days of Kilindi was not there."

" How was that, Khamis," we interrupted, " why was the harbour not there ? "

" Nay, Masters, be not so impatient.   Nigojia kidojo (wait a little).   Had you been silent awhile you would have heard, as my story went on, how it was that the harbour was first made."

Khamis was quite put out at our interruption, for he was a man who did not love to be hurried, but liked to take things in their proper order, and tell his story in his own way.

"Well, Khamis, tupa hadithi, tell your story as you please ; our tongues shall be still and all our ears shall be yours."

Khamis pretended not to notice what we had said. He stretched himself out on the ground and gazed round indifferently at the trees—at the cornfields—at the distant Fort—and remarked that we should have a storm before night.

" Nay, Khamis," cried the men, "the Masters wait for the story, their ears are stretched to hear it, and they will be dumb as stones."

After a pause sufficiently long to impress us with the magnitude of our offence in breaking in upon the story, he continued. " Well, Masters, Munia Pembe was a powerful king, and Kilindi was a rich country. He had servants and slaves in numbers, who used to bring down to the coast great caravans of ivory, oil and precious woods from the unknown heart of Africa.

" Then, too, he had dhows and boats in plenty, which carried his merchandise to Ungujia and Hindee, and brought back rich eastern stuffs and spices, and gold for ornaments from the Arabs and merchants. Queri, Masters, believe me, he was a very great king.

" Now, though he was rich and powerful, and had all that the world could give him, he was sorrowful and weary of his life.

"Once he had a beautiful son called Oumouri, who was the light of his house ; but one day, when he was swimming with his playfellows in the surf, a great fish had seized him and carried him away before their eyes. Since then the King's heart has known no rest, for God had given him no other children.

" ' What,' cried he, ' are my riches, my ships, and my palaces, when the son who was the joy of my heart is no more ! '

*   *   *   *   *   *

" Now after the King, the next man of power in the land of Kilindi was the Kadi Mwili-fetha, or the Golden

instruments and sang wild, weird songs which they had learnt in distant lands.

"Then, too, when Armi commanded them, they told the girls of the strange things they had seen in the distant countries and savage lands they had reached in their search for ivory and gold. They told strange tales of the countries they had seen in their travels; countries inhabited by savages who ate the enemies they killed in battle. Countries where there were great forests which were watered by rivers on whose banks lived people who wore no clothes, and had tails like apes. People who trained savage dogs to fight against their enemies and guard their homes in the dark recesses of a great forest which stretched far away towards the setting sun.

"And so the three grew up together in a friendship that was strong and true.

"Now one day the Kadi Mwili-fetha sent for his daughter, and Sophonea coming to him, said, 'Speak, father, for thy daughter is before thee, and heareth with an obedient heart.'

"And the Kadi answered and said:

"'My daughter, I have seen the strong love which has grown up between Karibu and thee. It makes mine heart glad to see it, for she is a pure maiden and true, and I love her almost as I love thee, mine own daughter. For

many moons a thought has lain at mine heart how both
our lives may be brighter and made more full of happiness
and content.   My daughter, though the freshness of my
youth is past, it has come to me that it were a good thing
to take to myself the mother of Karibu—the Bibi Raba—
for my wife.   She, too, has lost the first freshness of youth,
yet she is still pleasing to the sight, and has long looked
upon me with kindly eyes.   She would be a mother to
thee and Karibu alike, and we might all live together, in
this mine house, in happiness and peace.   And now, my
daughter, I have opened mine heart, and have shown thee
the thought which has lain there so long.   Speak, then,
all that is in thine heart, and tell me if this thing be
pleasing to thee.'

" ' Nay, father,' answered Sophonea, ' it is true that thy
first youth hath departed, but thou art not yet stricken in
years.   If thine heart is set on the Bibi Raba, I bow to thy
will, for thy happiness is mine.'

" ' Yet, my daughter,' answered the Kadi, 'though the
thought of this hath been with me long, a fear has come
over me lest perchance when the Bibi Raba came to mine
house she would not love thee, and then my heart would
break.'

" ' Fear not for me, my father,' said Sophonea, ' if thou
takest the Bibi Raba to wife I will be a dutiful and

obedient daughter to her, and she cannot help but love me.'

"'What thou sayest is true,' answered the Kadi, 'thou art so gentle and good, my child, that she cannot help but love thee.'

"So, when the days of the wedding-feast were over, Mwili-fetha took Raba for his wife, and brought her and Karibu home, and the four lived together in his palace by the sea.

"Now the Widow Raba had long coveted the riches of Mwili-fetha, and the high and honourable place she would take among the women of Kilindi as the Kadi's wife. She had therefore feigned great love for Sophonea, and had used every art to gain the affection of Mwili-fetha's daughter. But now that she was his wife and mistress of his house, she began to plot how she could ruin Sophonea, for at heart she hated her with a bitter hatred, and was jealous of her step-daughter because of her father's strong love for her. She thought, too, if she could but get rid of Sophonea that all the Kadi's riches and possessions would fall to her and her own daughter, Karibu. But she must be secret and wary, for she feared the Kadi, and dared not do anything openly against Sophonea. Day by day she watched, and waited, and plotted, till at last she had weaved a plan for her step-daughter's destruction.

So one day when the Kadi sat in the Temple of Judgment dispensing justice to the different applicants who sat on the pavement around the judgment-seat, Raba came out into the baraza of the palace, where Sophonea and Karibu were weaving the soft, coloured mats which the women of Kilindi to this day love to make.

"She spoke soft words to them and said, 'come, my daughters, the day is hot, put by the weaving. The karaffe (clove) harvest is now at its height; let us go into the field and see how the labourers proceed with their work.' The girls gladly threw their work aside, and Sophonea —always kind and good—thanked her step-mother for wishing to give them pleasure. But her very gentleness served but to increase Raba's hatred towards her, and hardened her heart against her to carry out the plan she had made for her destruction.

"The bearers carried them in their litter to the karaffe grove, and there, under the shade of the trees, the slaves spread gay-coloured mats and soft cushions, and Raba and the two girls reclined upon them. Fruit was brought them by the slaves; rich mellow plantains and juicy pine-apples from the plantations hard by, and luscious aromatic tasting mangoes and oranges from the fields and gardens of Ungujia. A servant by Raba's order then climbed a cocoa-nut tree and laid large green cocoa-nuts before them

—the tops of these being cut off furnished cups of sweet cool milk, a drink fit for kings.

" Now Raba had hidden a small but poisonous asp in her cloth and, unseen by anyone, she slipped it into her step-daughter's cup. Then raising the fruit in her hand she said, ' Let us drink, my daughters, of the cocoa-nut milk, and be grateful to the Gods for having given us a draught so sweet.'

" The girls raised the cocoa-nuts to their lips, but as they drank the snake slipped down the throat of Sophonea, who was immediately taken with strange pains and convulsions, and fell to the ground. With a cry of terror and affright Karibu raised her in her arms, while the slaves gathered round with sounds of fear and pity, for they all loved their young mistress. Raba, too, pretending to be full of astonishment at the strange sickness which had seized her step-daughter, called loudly for help. A litter was quickly brought, and Sophonea being laid softly in it, the poor girl, with moans and cries of pain and agony, was borne to her father's house followed by the weeping servants.

" As the Kadi sat in the Judgment Hall a slave rushed suddenly in, and throwing himself at his master's feet cried aloud, ' Rise up, oh Kadi, and come in haste, for Sophonea, thy beloved daughter, lies sick in thine house, with the pains of death upon her.'

"Quickly the Kadi rose up, and entering his house he beheld his daughter, supported by Karibu, lying on a couch, like one in death. With a cry of sorrow and despair he threw himself on his knees beside her and called wildly upon her to speak. But his voice fell on unheeding ears; for the the pains had again come upon her, and falling into a deep swoon she lay like one in a trance.

"The wise men of Kilindi and the medicine men from far and near were sent for, and they all talked learnedly and shook their heads wisely round the couch of Sophonea, but none of them could tell the nature of the malady which had come thus suddenly upon her.

"All that night the Kadi and Karibu watched in turn by the bedside of Sophonea; but alas! she grew worse and worse, and the convulsions became stronger and stronger.

"Raba watched, too, with words of sorrow and pity on her lips, but jealousy and hatred shone in her eyes, and feelings of triumph were in her heart at the success of her plot.

"The weary days dragged on and Sophonea grew weaker and weaker, till she seemed to be slowly fading away before their eyes.

"Now on the seventh day, as the Kadi watched by his daughter's couch, Karibu lay down to sleep, and as she slept dreamed a dream. A beautiful prince stood before her and said : ' I know, Karibu, that thou lovest thy sister ; give ear, therefore, to the words I speak, and follow the counsel I give thee. Thy sister Sophonea lies at the point of death, and her sickness has been caused by her wicked

"THE TWO WENT BEFORE THE KADI."

step-mother, the Bibi Raba. There is but one way by which thy sister may be made whole. Listen then, and let my words sink into thine heart. In the morning thou shalt go before the Kadi and bid him send thy sister and thee in a boat out to sea, and having done this he shall put his trust in the gods and wait for what shall befall.'

K

" When morning broke Karibu rose up and stood before the Kadi and told him her dream. Then was the Kadi filled with wrath against Raba, but he refused to let Karibu go, for his heart sank at the thought of losing both his daughters.

" ' What ! ' cried he ; ' is it not enough that the wife I took to comfort me in my old age has turned against me and made my house a house of mourning, without sending my daughter away, so that I shall not even see her die, and shall I lose thee also ? Nay, my daughter, I will not let thee go.'

" Karibu begged and prayed, but the Kadi only answered, ' I will not let thee go.' So Karibu, weeping, left the Kadi's presence and going to the young man Armi told him her dream and asked him to help her.

" Then the two went hand in hand before the Kadi and begged so earnestly, that at length a hope sprang up in his heart that perhaps good luck would come of it and Sophonea be healed. So at last he granted their prayer and a boat was got ready, and food for the girls was put into it.

" Next day the Kadi slaughtered cows and goats to propitiate the gods, and at night he and Armi secretly bearing Sophonea down to the sea-shore laid her in the boat, while Karibu took her place beside her sister. Sad

were their farewells, and bitter the tears they shed as
Mwili-fetha and Armi raised their hands above their
heads and besought the gods to watch over the helpless
girls and guide the boat which held them.

"Then they pushed the boat into the water, and the
breeze caught the sail and carried her on through the
darkness till she faded away from their sight. And Armi
led the heart-broken Kadi back to his house and abode
there with him.

* * * * * *

"The boat drifted out to sea with Sophonea lying still in
a trance and Karibu watching beside her. The tide took
them and carried them down the coast, and the winds and
waves caught the boat and tossed it to and fro, till Karibu
wept aloud in her loneliness and sang songs of lamentation
and farewell to her home and friends in Kilindi. The
fishermen of Pemba and Combro as they lay in their huts
heard her singing as the boat drifted by in the darkness;
and as they listened to the sweet and mournful sound of
her voice they thought that the 'Spirit of the Sea' passed
by, and hastened in the morning to light fresh lamps in her
temple and lay fresh offerings of fruit and flowers on her
altar. And the boat drifted on and on, the plaything of the
winds and waves. She drifted past islands and rocks
where the great seals lay basking in the sun, and they

blinked their eyes lazily as the boat sailed by, asking each other who these strange creatures were. Then they barked and growled among themselves, till Karibu in fear clasped her sister and cowered terror-stricken in the bottom of the boat. She did not know that the seal is a kindly, harmless creature, and does not hurt people—she did not understand, Masters, that seals, like a good many other people in the world, bark and growl a great deal but mean no harm by it. The dolphins and bonitos played and dived in front of the boat as much as to say, 'You cannot catch us,' and the flying fish flew like clouds of silver over their heads. But still Sophonea lay in a trance, and the boat drifted on and on. They passed the islands and away from the land, and out on to the wide ocean where the great green icebergs bowed their heads and plunged and sailed before the breeze. Among them Karibu could see the great whales, which looked far off like the black hulls of ships, as they rose and fell in the water, and spouted up clouds of spray and foam—till she feared lest they should upset the boat.

"Here, too, flocks of birds filled the air. The great white albatross—the holy bird which brings the breeze— sailed in the air with outstretched wings, far above their heads, while the greedy Molly hawks and gulls followed the boat and quarrelled and screamed around them.

The wave birds, the little stormy petrels, skimmed over the waves and darted in and out about the boat, like big black and white butterflies. So all the birds of the air followed them and watched them, and they too, like the seals, wondered who the two girls could be.

"They drifted south till a great storm arose and drove them northward: the sky became black as ink and the wind raged and howled around them. The waves rose up like mountains and swept the boat along while the spray drove over them in showers. The thunder crashed and roared, the lightning lit up the sky, and the boat shook and strained and groaned as she bounded before the storm. Karibu, with the sleeping Sophonea in her arms, crouched down in terror, and prayed aloud to the gods to watch over and protect them.

" For three days and nights the storm raged around them, till at last, worn out with watching, Karibu fell asleep. How long she slept she knew not, but when she awoke she found the storm had ceased and the sun was shining bright and warm upon her. Looking round she saw that the boat had drifted towards an island, and was lying in a beautiful bay, quite still upon the glassy sea. The bay lay stretched out before her like the arc of a bow, and the soft swell lapped up upon the golden strand and fell back into the sea in tiny ripples with a sound like laughter. The cocoa-nut trees grew down to the water's edge, and their leaves waved slowly to and fro in the soft morning breeze, while the low hum of insects filled the air, and all the world seemed bright and beautiful.

"Ah! how peaceful the scene seemed to her eyes after drifting so long on the ocean, tossed by the winds and waves. Karibu rose up and ate and drank, the first food she had eaten for many days, and as she leaned over the side of the boat to wash the cup, she saw deep down in the water below what seemed to her to be an enchanted garden at the bottom of the sea.

"There were great red and yellow and purple wreaths of sea-weed which grew up like trees from the snow-white sand below, and as they moved to and fro with the tide it seemed almost as if their branches were swayed by the breeze. In and out among them swam gold and silver fish, chasing each other round and round and playing among their branches.

"Allah! was anything ever so beautiful! And as she gazed into the depths below, slowly out from a cave of coral at the bottom of the sea swam a beautiful Diamond Fish which glittered like a jewel in the sun. Up and up it swam towards her till it reached the surface, and looking at her with human eyes, asked, 'Who art thou, fair maiden, and from whence hast thou come?'

"'We are two maidens of Kilindi,' answered Karibu, 'and my sister lies here like one in death.'

"Then she told the story of Sophonea's sickness, of her dream, and of how they had drifted far across the ocean to the island.

"'I will help thee,' said the Fish, and diving to the

bottom of the sea, it brought up in its mouth a little sand and laid it in the hand of Karibu.

"'Now,' said the Fish, 'thou shalt make "uji upasi" (thin porridge) of pili-pili and rice, and putting the sand into it, thou shalt give it to thy sister to drink, and she will be healed.'

"' And what reward dost thou demand for thy service ?' asked Karibu.

"' At sun-down I will return to claim my reward,' answered the Fish, as he dived down again to the bottom of the sea.

" Karibu obeyed the Fish's commands, and making the uji, she poured it down the throat of Sophonea. Violent convulsions immediately came over the sick girl, until Karibu feared lest her sister was dying ; but when the convulsions had reached their height, the snake which she had swallowed at last slid from her mouth and fell into the sea.   Soon the trance left her ; her blood resumed its flow, and life came back to her once more. As Karibu stood watching her she opened her eyes and awoke, and the two girls wept together and kissed each other in deep joy. Then Karibu told her sister all that had happened, and how the Fish who had helped her was to come at sun-down and claim his reward.

" All day long they sat talking together in the boat, and wondering what would happen. In fear and trembling they watched as the sun grew low in the heaven for the coming of the Diamond Fish, for they knew not what the reward he would ask might be. Anxiously they watched the sun as he dropped like a ball of fire into the sea, and as he disappeared a sudden movement behind them startled the girls, and turning round quickly they saw standing before them a beautiful Prince.

"Sophonea started up in astonishment, crying, 'It is Oumouri, the playmate of my childhood, and the Prince of my dreams!'

"'Yes, I am Oumouri, thou hast not forgotten me!' cried the Prince, clasping her in his arms.

"'Ay! I remember thee too,' cried Karibu, 'thou art he who came to me in my dream, and told me how I could save my sister.'

"'Yea,' answered Oumouri, 'I am he who appeared to thee in a dream the night thy sister lay dying; my thanks be with thee for ever for listening to the words I spoke, for thou hast saved both her and me.'

"Then Oumouri leaned over the boat and called aloud, and up from the bottom of the sea swam a cloud of gold and silver fish. And by the Prince's command they fastened long wreaths of sea-weed to the boat, and taking the ends in their mouths they drew it rapidly through the water, away from the island, and out to sea.

"And Oumouri sat in the stern of the boat with Sophonea's hand in his, and told the girls his story. He told them that the big fish who had carried him away was a wicked Magician, and how when he was dragged under the water he had lost his senses, and awoke to find himself transformed into a Diamond Fish on the shores of the island of Lanka.

"The cruel Magician had power over his body, but the Sea-God had had pity upon him, and had allowed his spirit to appear to Sophonea in her dreams. The God had told him that if he could but restore life to one of his fellow-creatures he would be able to resume his own form once more and escape from the power of the Magician. The Magician had shut him up in a coral cave at the bottom of the sea, and he had not been able to escape from the bay. As the years went on, and no human beings had come over the sea to the island he had despaired of ever regaining his form and returning to Kilindi, but from time to time he had appeared to Sophonea. His spirit had seen Raba's cruel act to her step-daughter, and he had thought that by this plan of the boat he might save both Sophonea and himself. The Sea-God had helped him, and had commanded the winds and waves to bring the boat to the island of Lanka.

"The sand he had given to Karibu was the Magician's magic sand and possessed marvellous powers of healing; and when Sophonea came back to life, at sun-down he had been freed from the power of the Magician.

"And so, drawn by the gold and silver fishes, the boat sailed back to Kilindi.

"The people in the city saw the boat coming and

hurried down to the sea-shore to see who the strangers could be. But the fish swam quickly on round the head-land and past the city, and ran the boat upon the shore with such force that it cut deep into the land. And, Masters," continued Khamis, " it was by the boat that the far-famed harbour of Kilindi was made.

" Immediately the boat struck the shore the gold and silver fish regained their forms, and became men ; for they, too, were youths of Kilindi who had long been under the spell of the wicked Magician.

" The strangers were soon recognized, and messengers were quickly sent to carry the news to the King and the Kadi, while the people, with joyful acclamations, accom-panied them to the King's palace.

" The whole people of the city had assembled before the palace, for the news of their return had spread abroad. And a great cry of joy arose from the multitude when the aged King, Munia Pembe, came down the steps of the palace, and with tears of joy fell on the neck of his long-lost son Oumouri.

" The Kadi, too, was sent for to his house where he had shut himself up alone with Armi, mourning for the loss of his daughter. And soon the two came to the King's palace and clasped the wanderers in their arms.

*   *   *   *   *   *

"Then a great banquet was spread, and the whole of the King's household sat down to eat and listened to their wonderful story. And when the tale was told abroad the people laughed and sang, and there was great joy that night in Kilindi. For six days the whole city feasted and rejoiced, and on the seventh day Oumouri took Sophonea for his wife, while Armi married Karibu.

"This," said Khamis Parri, "is the legend; some call it the story of Mwili-fetha, and others the story of Kilindi."

"And what became of Raba?" asked Binza, who always wanted to know everything.

"Yes," exclaimed all the men, "tell us, Khamis, what became of the wicked step-mother. The Kadi's vengeance surely fell upon her?"

"Well," answered Khamis, "I will tell you. That night when the girls started on their long journey in the boat, the Kadi returned to his house to find that Raba, fearing his vengeance, had fled, taking with her all the jewels she could carry. By offering a large reward she persuaded a boatman to row her across secretly to the island of Pemba, hoping to hide herself there and escape punishment. But in the night a storm arose which wrecked the boat, and Raba never reached the shore, but was overwhelmed in the raging sea."

"Ah!" murmured Abedi, "it was but right that Raba

should perish, for she was too wicked to live. How is it, M'seh Raschid, that while our mothers are so kind, our step-mothers are often so cruel?"

Raschid scratched his head and seemed puzzled what to say, but never liking to appear unable to answer anything, he tried to turn the question aside by saying to me,

"Do white men, Master, in Ulayia often take to themselves a second wife?"

"Queri, Raschid, indeed they do," I answered laughingly, "and sometimes not more happily than Mwili-fetha. There are Rabas in every country, Raschid, who are unkind to their husband's children; still, there are many step-mothers who are kind."

"That is true, Master," remarked some of the men near me, who immediately began to talk about some of the step-mothers they knew, but from the remarks they made about them I gathered that step-mothers were not much appreciated in Zanzibar.

After some little talk, Mr. Stanley announced to the men he had at last decided that at the beginning of the next week he intended to start a second time for the Nyanza. They hailed the news with joy, for the Zanzibaris do not love to stay long in one place, and are never so happy as when they are on the march. Noisy shouts of pleasure, therefore, greeted this announcement, and everyone talked excitedly about it.   Some wondered, whether Stairs would return from Ugarrowa's in time to go with us ; what path we were likely to take, and whether we would find plenty of food on the way.   Others questioned whether we should have much fighting with the natives ; how and when we should at last find Emin Pasha, and twenty other things, all of which they talked about at the top of their voices.

Everyone had something to say or some suggestion to make, and they were still talking excitedly when the night fell and we returned to the Fort.

That night we sat with our leader talking over various plans and the prospects of the march before us.   We could hear our men outside talking and laughing round their fires, some of them were even singing.   Their sadness of the morning seemed all swept away by the delightful prospect of once more being on the march.

It was not that they did not grieve truly for the death of their comrades, it was not that their hearts were un-kindly, but it was merely because they were like children, and each new feeling soon swept away the last.   For these simple, laughter-loving Negroes are most of them in heart, after all, nothing but grown-up children.

CHAPTER VIII.

THE STORY OF THE CAT AND THE RAT.

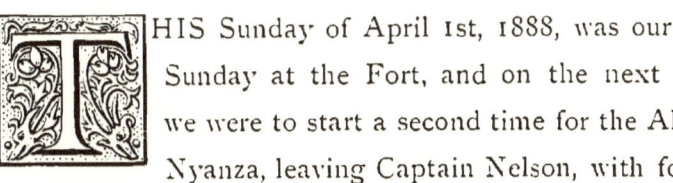HIS Sunday of April 1st, 1888, was our last
Sunday at the Fort, and on the next day
we were to start a second time for the Albert
Nyanza, leaving Captain Nelson, with forty-
five men and some women and children, to look after the
Fort while we were away.

Captain Stairs had not yet returned from Ugarrowa's
with the sick men we had left behind there. When
he started we expected him back in thirty-five days,
but he had now been gone forty-five days and we had
heard no tidings of him. What had happened to him
we could not imagine. Had he and his little band of
men lost their way and perished in that dark forest?
Had hostile natives lain in wait for them and killed
them by the way? Had he ever even reached Ugarrowa's
village? These and a score of others were the questions
we asked each other as we anxiously waited his arrival.

The pleasure of again being on the march and returning to the Lake was greatly spoilt for me by his not being with us. After our leader he was the most useful man in the expedition, and worked well with Negroes and Europeans alike. I myself was greatly attached to him, for we thought alike on so many subjects, and had never had an angry word together. Whenever he was away I always missed him, for there is no place like Africa for teaching one the value of a good and true comrade. I knew, moreover, how disappointed he would be at having missed going back to the Lake and meeting Emin, and how, with his love of movement and action, he would fret his life out at the Fort, if indeed he ever reached it.

But it was of no use repining, for we could not wait for him. We could not rest; we could not think of lingering by the way; we could not turn aside until we had carried help to Emin; for had he not written in despair to the people of England, " Help us quickly, or we perish."

So all that week we went on working hard to have everything ready for a start.

Our Fort was now snug and safe for Captain Nelson and his men, and it would be almost impossible for the savages ever to get into it. We had overhauled and put in order all our guns, and had given a fresh supply of ammunition to our men in case we should have fighting on the way. They had got large supplies of flour ground ready for the road, and all the boxes and loads had been distributed to the different men to carry. The boat, upon which depended so much, had also been got in readiness. It was in twelve pieces, and each piece was tied to a long pole and carried on the shoulders of two men. Then, for the last few days, I had been busily engaged in making new oars for the boat from small trees which we cut down in the forest. It was our first attempt at making oars, and Uledi, the coxswain of the the boat, and I felt immensely proud of them.

We had forgotten nothing, and when that Sunday morning broke all our preparations were finished.

In the morning Dr. Parke and I sat in the veranda of our mud hut and patched and darned our tattered clothes, for we wanted to cut a respectable appearance when we met Emin Pasha's people.

The clothes we brought with us from home were nearly finished, but we were clever in making others. I remember Dr. Parke made himself a wonderful pair of trousers out of an old blue and white-checked bed coverlet. He covered his umbrella, too, with the same stuff, to match his trousers, and very smart he looked with them. He

L

was just like the "Blackamoor" in "Strewel Peter" who
walked out with his umbrella to take the air, and was
shouted at and pursued by the naughty little boys until
the great Magrippa caught them and dipped them all
into the ink. But the little Negro boys in our camp
were well behaved, and saw nothing to laugh at in our
Doctor's appearance. On the contrary, he looked very
grand and smart in their eyes, and when, later on, we
reached the Lake all the natives thought he must be a
king, or at least a prince, and brought him presents of
chickens and eggs, all on account of his blue and white
umbrella and trousers.

I worked away at my clothes, too, and patched up the
holes in my stockings with bits of cloth from an old
coat. And then I made myself two pairs of shoes, for
I was an excellent cobbler. I made them out of the
skin of a black and white spotted cow, and I left the
hair on, so that I, too, should have a gay appearance like
the Doctor, for I did not like to be outdone by him!
And so we worked on, until by the afternoon we had
patched and mended ourselves from head to foot.

Doubtless, in Europe, we should have cut a sorry
figure, and appeared to be "mere things of shreds and
patches," but we ourselves thought we were splendid,
and were ready to face the whole world now that we

were mended up. We walked proudly through the Fort with a conscious feeling of satisfaction that our men were all admiring our appearance, for we felt that we couldn't possibly have looked better if we had been rigged out from head to foot by the best London tailor and shoemaker.

And why was it that we were so satisfied? I will tell you; it was simply because we had made everything ourselves.

You will perhaps laugh at this, children, but it is true for all that. You need to go through trials and hardships far away from home; to be shut away from civilization for long months in the heart of an African forest; to be forced to depend upon yourselves for everything you eat or wear to realize how little we can be happy and satisfied with.

* * * * * *

There were not many men under the tree that afternoon when I strolled up with my pipe and sat down at the edge of the forest for the usual Sunday gossip. Raschid, our head chief, was there however, and Murabo and several others. Mr. Stanley and Dr. Parke were still in their huts, finishing little jobs or writing up their journals, while most of the men were preparing and packing up their food for the morrow's march.

After some talk one of the men began to speak about

being worried the night before by the rats running over him in his hut. Now as we extended our cultivation and our granaries had become full, so the rats about the Fort had increased and multiplied in proportion, until at last they had become a positive plague. They often disturbed us at night by scampering over us, or dropping down upon our beds from the rafters of the roof. We were wishing we had some cats about the Fort to kill them, and I asked Raschid how it was that while we saw so many dogs in the native huts we never saw any cats. He told me that even in the villages near the town of Zanzibar the people could never keep their cats, for they always roamed away into the country and became wild, preferring to hunt for their own food.

"You know, I suppose, Master," here remarked Nelson's boy, Osmani, "why it is that the cat and the rat are such enemies?"

"No, Osmani," I answered; "were they not always so?"

"Certainly not, B'wana," he replied; "they were once great friends. Shall I tell you how through the greed and laziness of the rat they first fell out?"

"Aywah," exclaimed the men, "tell us about it!" and, as we settled ourselves comfortably down to listen to the story, Osmani began.

*   *   *   *   *   *

"Once upon a time, long ago, Paka the cat and Pania the rat lived together as friends on the island of Myoti, or, as some call it, Maori. It was one of those small islands which lie together, like a string of beads, to the south of Ungujia. These islands were small and were covered with woods, but were seldom visited by human

"LET US LEAVE THIS ISLAND."

beings, who lived in the larger islands of Mouali, Combro, Pemba, or on the mainland of Ungujia.

"And it was here that Paka the cat and Pania the rat dwelt together alone in close friendship. They lived in a small, dry, sandy cave in the rocks, and made themselves warm, comfortable beds of dry leaves and grass.

"They led a pleasant easy life, for there was plenty for them to eat. The cat caught birds in the trees, and the rat lived upon nuts and the roots of the mahogo (manioc) plant which grew wild in great abundance on the island.

"Now after they had lived together many years on the island of Myoti, the rat one day said, 'Let us leave this island, Paka, and go to the island of Mouali, in which dwell human beings, I am tired of the life here alone; let us go and see how the children of men live.'

"'To be sure, Pania,' answered the cat; 'I am willing to go, but between us and Mouali rolls the deep salt sea. How shall we cross it, for the tide runs strong, and we cannot swim so far?'

"'Let us build a boat,' answered the rat. 'We will dig up a big mahogo root which we can scoop out and make into a canoe.'

"'Queri,' said the cat, 'we will try.'

"After searching for some time they found a mahogo root which the rat said was large enough, and digging it up they set to work to scoop it out.

"The rat with his sharp teeth bit out pieces from the inside, while the cat scratched and scratched at it with his long claws, until, after several days' work, between them they managed to make the mahogo root into a canoe. It was very thin and frail, and the cat wondered much whether it would safely hold them.

"'Have no fear,' said the rat, 'it will carry us well;

"THEY SET TO WORK TO SCOOP IT OUT."

we will make some oars to paddle it along, and you will see we shall reach Mouali safely.'

" Then they pushed the mahogo root into the water and started off on their voyage to Mouali.

"But it was farther than they thought and the tide ran strong against them.

"The rat, who was lazy, soon got tired and hungry and, laying down his paddle began to eat pieces of the mahogo-root canoe. The cat, however, who was sitting in front, went on paddling diligently until at last he was out of breath. Turning round he saw that the rat had put down his paddle and was greedily nibbling away at the bottom of the boat.

"'What are you doing,' asked the cat, 'am I to do all the work? Take care or you will eat a hole in the boat.'

"'Nay,' answered the rat, 'I stopped but for a moment to take breath, I am hungry, too, and am only eating a little of the mahogo.'

"The cat was satisfied and went on paddling until he was tired out, but the canoe seemed to him to move very slowly, and looking round again he saw that the rat was still nibbling at the canoe.

"This time he was very angry and cried 'You lazy, greedy fellow! you not only leave me to do all the work, but in your greediness you will make a hole in the boat and we shall both be drowned.'

"The rat, somewhat frightened by the cat's anger, begged his pardon, and hurriedly taking up his paddle he began to row again.

"And so they worked on together for awhile, until the boat was half-way between the two islands. But soon the rat's greediness again got the better of him, and once more he began to nibble at the boat, until he had gnawed the bottom so thin that the water burst in and the boat began to fill.

"AND SO THEY WORKED ON TOGETHER."

"The cat started up with an exclamation of fury and anger and tried to seize the rat, but before he could do so the boat sank and left them both struggling in the water.

"'You good-for-nothing fellow,' spluttered the cat as he rose to the surface and swam towards the rat, 'you have eaten the boat, and now I will revenge myself by eating you.'

" 'Wait,' gasped the rat, 'you cannot eat me here, for the salt water will get down your throat, and make your stomach sick ; let us swim on to the island and when we land you can eat me.'

" 'Very well,' said the cat, 'you swim on, and I will swim behind to see that you do not escape.'

" VERY WELL, YOU SWIM ON."

" So on they swam until they had reached the shore.

" ' Now,' cried the cat, as they scrambled on land, ' now I will make a meal off you, and punish you for your greediness and treachery.'

" ' Wait,' answered the rat, at his wits' end what to do ; ' be not so impatient, there is plenty of time to eat me, let me but shake the salt water from my sides, I shall taste much better without salt. Sit down in the sun and dry your own coat, I shall be ready for you very soon.'

" The cat agreed, and, sitting down, began to dry himself in the sun.

" Meanwhile the rat, pretending to dry himself, began scratching a hole in the ground as fast as he could,

" BUT THE RAT SHOT INTO THE HOLE."

thinking if he only had time to make it deep enough, he might even yet get out of the cat's clutches.

" The cat looked round suspiciously and asked him what he was doing, but the rat assured him that he was only shaking the water off his back, and the cat, satisfied with his answer, went on cleaning himself in the sun.

" The rat went on scratching hard, and every now and

then peeped round to see that the cat was not looking, until at last he had made quite a deep hole and paused on the edge to take breath.

"Just then the cat, who was now quite dry, made a spring at him crying, 'Now, you treacherous friend, I will eat you up!'

"But the rat shot into the hole and escaped from his clutches.

"And from that time to this," continued Osmani, "all cats have been enemies with the whole tribe of rats and their cousins, the mice.

"So whenever you see a cat prowling round, you will know, Master, that it is looking for its enemy the rat ; for every cat tells her kittens the story of Pania the rat's treachery to Paka the cat, and bids them never to cease hunting for him."

"Is that really so, Osmani ?" we asked.

"Queri," interrupted Binza, "it is, I know, a true story, for I have heard it told many times before. I wish, though, the cat had caught the rat, for he deserved to die for playing his friend so dirty a trick. The cat was a great fool not to see through his trick, he should not have waited, but should have eaten him up, 'chop! chop!'"

"Ay," said Raschid, as usual trying to point a moral

to every tale, "see what a bad thing is laziness, and the greediness which always goes with it, and how often it kills friendship between us. Do we not see greediness and laziness about us every day, and what it leads to? Are there not 'goee goees' (idlers) in our camp who are never to be found when work is to be done, who try to shift their work, as the rat did, on to their comrades' shoulders, but are ever at hand when the time for giving potio (rations of food) draws near? It is the 'goee goees' who in the camp or on safari who make bad blood among us, and give more trouble to the Masters than all the rest. And greed of gain and money is just the same thing, and works the same mischief to us all. It was greed of gain which turned Said Said, the Sultan of Muscat, against our own Said Burghash his brother, and brought war upon Ungujia. It is greed which changes the merchants of Ungujia into slave and ivory raiders, like Tippu Tib and Kilonga-longa, who have turned this land into a desert. Why Masters, it was through greed that men first became monkeys."

"You don't mean to say so, Raschid!" I exclaimed. "Is there a story about that too?"

"Queri, Masters," he replied, "it is called the story of Kema na Niaan (the monkey and the ape); it is a common story which we tell our children in Zanzibar, every Zanzibari knows it. Hyia Omari, you have two children and have often told it to them, I am sure, you speak and tell us the story."

"No, M'seh, you know the story better than I, you tell it to us."

The old man was quite pleased at having pointed a moral, as he thought, so aptly, and nothing loth to follow it up, he began the story without more persuasion.

"Years ago in the island of Pemba there lived two friends called Makasara and Hassara. Makasara was a big strong man, and Hassara was small and weak.'

"They had a little shamba (farm) where they used to grow cloves, but they were idle and worthless, and loved better to steal the fruit and corn from their neighbours' fields than to cultivate their own crops.

"Near them lived an old man called Kibongi. He had plantations of cloves, cocoa-nuts, and mangoes, and large fields of corn and potatoes. He was a very rich man, but miserly, and lived alone on his shamba with an old slave woman who used to look after his house and cook his food.

"One day as Makasara passed by he saw the old man sitting on the floor of his hut counting over his money, which he took from a large bag. He crept quietly round

"EAGERLY HE WATCHED THE OLD MAN."

the hut and watched him through a chink in the wall, and as he saw the heaps of gold and silver his heart was consumed with greed for it. Eagerly he watched the old man, who, when he had finished counting it, put it back into the bag and hid it in a hole in the floor at one of the corners of the hut. Then Makasara crept silently away, and told Hassara all that he had seen. He told him that there was enough to keep them in comfort and idleness for the rest of their lives if they could only steal it.

" Hassara, who was timid, was afraid that they might be found out. But Makasara told him how easy it would be to get it, for the old man slept alone in his hut.

" At last he persuaded Hassara to help him, and they decided to steal the old man's treasure, and made a secret place in their hut in which to hide it. In the dead of night, therefore, they stole up to Kibongi's hut, and opening one of the windows they crept into the room. The old man was lying on his bed and seemed to be sound asleep, so they crept past him to the corner of the hut where the treasure was hidden, and began to dig up the mud floor with their knives. But just as they had found it and were dragging it out of the hole, the gold gave forth a chinking noise, and at the sound the old man awoke. He started up in his bed, and seeing, by the moonlight, the robbers making off with his treasure, he called out 'm'wivi! m'wivi!' (thieves! thieves!) and shouted loudly for help.

"In rushed the old slave woman, and she too set up a shrill screaming, but Makasara seized the old man by the throat and stabbed him to the heart, while Hassara,

".ALL JOINED IN THE CHASE."

thrusting the old woman aside, made off with the treasure, followed by Makasara.

"Kibongi's cries for help and the screams of the old woman had, however, awakened the people of the village near by, who came running from every side to see what had befallen, and as the robbers ran away from the hut, bearing the treasure between them, they were seen by the villagers, who all joined in the chase to hunt down the murderers. But the robbers ran so fast that they distanced their pursuers and managed to reach the forest. And so they ran on and on through the night until they were tired out, and when morning broke they climbed up into a big tree and hid themselves among its branches. There they stayed, for they were afraid to come down from the tree for fear of being seen by the people and being killed by them.

"They dared not leave the forest, and were afraid even to light a fire to cook their food, lest their hiding place would be discovered, so they fed upon nuts and wild fruit and roots.

"The days passed by and grew into weeks and months, until from being up in the tree so long, and holding on to the branches, their feet became like hands. Their fingers grew like claws from digging up roots, and, as as their clothes wore out, hair began to grow all over their bodies. Their mouths, too, became large and wide and their teeth long and sharp, from cracking nuts and eating roots. So day by day they became more and more ugly, until at last they began to lose their power of speaking and could only make chattering noises.

"One day they discovered that each had a white spot in the middle of his back, at which they became very frightened, and tried to hide it.

"THEY FED UPON NUTS AND WILD FRUITS AND ROOTS"

"THEY FOUND THAT THEY HAD BECOME MONKEYS."

"But slowly out from the white spots grew long hairy tails, until one morning when they woke up they found that they had become monkeys. Makasara was changed into a big, savage ape, and Hassara into a little, chattering monkey.

"And that Master," concluded Raschid, "is how monkeys were first made. The savage baboons, and gorillas, and apes are the murderers and felons, and the small monkeys are the thieves and liars. And all this, Master, as I said before, came from greed."

"Queri," murmured the men, "that is the truth ; the old man has Akili, and speaks well.

"What you say, Raschid," I exclaimed, "is strange, for we have a learned man in Ulayia, called Bwana Darwin, and he tells us that men have sprung from monkeys ; that agrees not with your story."

"Then, Bwana Bubarika," answered Raschid contemptuously, "Bwana Darwin must be without sense, for who ever heard of monkeys becoming men ? I never have, and I am now an old man. The Wa-Swahili are not the only people who believe that wicked men are changed into animals ; why, even the Wa-Shenzi (Pagans) know that hyenas and leopards, and other fierce beasts, have once been evil men."

"Well, Raschid," I replied, "I think that Bwana Darwin

probably knows better than you do, and is more likely to be right, for he is a real fundi and speaks with Akilli. And he has books, too, Raschid, by hundreds, books which have been written by other fundis as clever as himself."

Raschid seemed staggered by this ; for he thought that evidence coming from books must be right, and he scarcely knew what to say. The men, too, looked at each other in doubt, as if they hardly knew which of the two, Raschid or I, was most likely to be right.

But Murabo, the wit of the party, covered Raschid's confusion, and came to his rescue by exclaiming, with a twinkle in his eye, " Eh, Wallah Bwana, you may both be right. It is quite possible that white men may have sprung from monkeys, but we all know that black men have not. Raschid, our father, is not mistaken."

We smiled at this suggestion of the inferiority of white men's origin, and I laughingly retorted, "Nay, Murabo, I do not think that that is likely, for you must allow that the black man's nose and mouth is much more like a monkey's than a white man's."

" It may be so, Bwana," he answered, "yet if you take any monkey and thrust his hair aside with your fingers you will find that his skin is always white."

As he said this he pulled down his lower eyelid with his

finger and looked sideways at me in such a comical manner that we all burst out laughing, and I had to admit that he had the best of the argument.

And so, with a good deal of chaff and laughter at my discomfiture, we returned to the Fort, from which for the last half hour the sound of horns and drums had reached our ears faintly across the corn-fields.

As we entered the gate we found that all was noise and laughter. Drums and horns were sounding, while one of the men was strutting about in imitation of General Mathews, the head of the troops in Zanzibar, pretending to drill a body of men who were got up fantastically in skins and feathers. He gave the words of command, " Shoulder arms," " Present arms," " Stand at ease," in broken English, and made the men go through the most absurd figures, much to the amusement of us all. They were all perfectly wild with excitement at the thoughts of marching on the morrow and reaching the open country, where there would be plenty of good food to eat.

We stood on one of the watch-towers looking at them all dancing and singing until darkness came on, and we went to our huts to eat our frugal supper of porridge, the last I was to eat at the Fort.

Though I was glad to be on the move again I could not help feeling a little sad when I went to bed that night at

the thought of leaving the place which we had made
ourselves, and which had sheltered us so long.

* * * * * *

At daybreak next morning, when the trumpet sounded,
most of us were already astir, packing up the few things
which we had left out over-night. The men were drawn
up in companies in the square yard, those who were going
with us on the one side, and those who were remaining
with Captain Nelson on the other.

When all the loads were given out, and everyone was
ready to start, Mr. Stanley stepped out before the men
and said a few helpful, kindly words to all.

To the men who were going to the Lake he spoke of
reaching Emin Pasha and of the march before us. To
those who were remaining at the Fort he said farewell,
promising a speedy return and urging them to be obedient
and faithful to Captain Nelson, and to have all things in
order when he returned from the Lake.

This they all cheerfully promised, and the final farewells
being said, amid many expressions of good-will from
all, the trumpet sounded, the flags were unfurled, and
each man, picking up his load, marched away from the
Fort.

I brought up the rear and was the last to leave.
Captain Nelson accompanied us to the edge of the forest

and stood waving his hat to us until a turn in the road hid him from our view, and we left the Peaceful Fort behind.

It had really been to us, up to that time, a peaceful fort in spite of the hard work and many troubles we had had there. There had been a certain element of home about it, and I could not but experience a feeling of regret at leaving it behind. My fellow officers returned to it afterwards and lived there a long time, but I myself did not come back, long months of imprisonment were in store for me, and I never saw it again.

*   *   *   *   *   *

This, children, is the end of my little book, and I hope I have been able to interest you in what I have told you. If it did not take too long I should like to have told you more about our life ; how we found and rescued Emin Pasha, and brought him with his people safely down to the coast. I should like to have told you, too, something of how we lived happily for months in little grass huts among the hospitable " Stranger People," the Wa-huma, or Shepherd Kings, who dwelt among their flocks and herds on the breezy, grassy uplands near the great lakes of Central Africa. A kindly people, living in all simplicity and in happy ignorance of everything belonging to the great restless world outside. Not knowing what hurry and bustle is, but living as their fathers and grandfathers have lived before them, unchanging for a hundred generations.

But I must say farewell to you now. As I write these words, and think of those days that we passed there, a kindly feeling of sympathy and gratitude rises up in my heart for those simple, trustful people who live contented with their lot in that rich, fertile country in the heart of Africa—people who showed us so much kindness and hospitality. My thoughts go back, too, to our faithful Zanzibaris who stood by us so loyally and worked for us so well in our long and terrible march across Africa. And this little book contains some of the stories they told us in the middle of the great dark forest.

CHISWICK PRESS :—C. WHITTINGHAM AND CO., TOOKS COURT, CHANCERY LANE.

www.ingramcontent.com/pod-product-compliance
Lightning Source LLC
Chambersburg PA
CBHW020604030726
47497CB00007B/2077